A Clean Sweep

by

Sara Bourgeois

Chapter One

"You have got to be kidding me," Annika said as I drained another margarita. "Please tell me you're joking."

Remy and Brody were at the archives doing whatever they did there while Annika and I had a girls' night. Remy had looked like he hadn't wanted to leave me in the state I was in, but Annika assured him she could handle it and pushed them out the door.

Thorn had left the night before to go see his ex-wife with promises to call me as soon as he could. I hadn't heard from him much. He wasn't sure what was going on, but he'd said he'd get to the bottom of it and make things right. Whatever that meant.

"I'm not joking. Apparently, she showed back up in town with a kid that looks just like Thorn."

"I mean, that doesn't mean it's his," Annika offered.

"Given that he could just get a DNA test, I don't see why she would lie," I said.

"Because some women are able to convince men not to get a DNA test," Annika said. "Maybe she's one of those super manipulative types. I could put a curse on her."

"We can't do that. She's the mother of a child. Probably Thorn's child. Oh, gawd," I said and took Annika's margarita from her hand. "Can you even imagine what it's going to be like if they get back together and stay here?"

"They're not getting back together," Annika said. "Did he say something like that? That's crazy."

"He didn't, but I'm just... I don't know. I'm all messed up about this. I mean, if they can work things out, isn't getting back together what's best for the little girl? Wouldn't that be the right thing for him to do?"

"People don't do stuff like that," Annika said. "They don't just drop everything and get back together for their kids. This isn't the 1950s"

"Thorn would do something like that. He does the right thing, Annika. That's who he is. You know it as well as I do," I said.

"Let's make another pitcher of margaritas," Annika said as she stood up and pulled me off the couch. "We'll make enough for the guys too. I'm sure they'll be done with their research soon. I doubt Remy will stay away for any longer than he absolutely has to."

"I don't know that it's a good idea for me to go getting drunk off my butt right now," I said.

"Why not? If any time is a good time for you to get drunk off your butt, I'd say it's now."

The next morning, I woke up with a pounding headache. Only after a few seconds of lying in bed wishing I could go back to sleep, I realized the pounding wasn't in my head. It was someone pounding on my front door.

My breath caught in my throat as I thought back to Grey banging away on the garage just before dawn. The garage that now stood half-finished at the top of my driveway. Could it be him back to finish me off?

Surely that wouldn't be the case. Meri had whipped up a spell that would let us see if it was him even if he was in a different form. I said I should go after him so he couldn't kill anyone else.

Meri said I should not go on a cross-country trek to find a cursed shifter serial killer. He said it was too risky, and that I might reveal to the federal government that I had powers they would like to obtain for their own purposes. But at least if he came back, Grey wouldn't be able to hide his identity from me.

The pounding on the door started again. I reached behind me to Meri's usual sleeping spot and found him gone.

That mystery was solved seconds later when he streaked into the room and jumped on the bed. "It's a bunch of people in baggy clothes drinking coffee and carrying filming equipment," Meri said. "Not a serial killer. Just annoying."

"What?" I asked and pushed myself out of bed.

I thought about getting dressed, but instead grabbed the robe I'd hung on the back of the bedroom door. After I'd tied the coral terry fabric around myself, I made my way out of the bedroom and down the stairs to the front door.

Sure enough, when I opened it, there was a motley crew of young men with one woman in the back. "Cool hair," she said from behind the guys in front of her.

"Thanks," I said. "Uh, can I help you?"

"Actually, we were hoping no one was here," the one in the front with the Harry Potter glasses and black goatee said.

"What?" I asked and considered slamming the door.

"Let me start over. I'm Kurt Holmes," Goatee said. "You might have heard of me."

"I have no idea who you are," I said dryly.

"From the show *Ghost Seekers*," the one in the back with long curly blond hair and a Grateful Dead t-shirt spoke up.

"We wanted to investigate this house," Kurt said. "We were kind of hoping it was abandoned."

"Does it look abandoned?" I asked.

No one responded.

"I mean, my car is parked in the driveway," I said and waved toward it.

"We thought it was just an old broken-down car left behind by whoever lived here last," the guy with the camera in his hands said.

"My car is not that bad," I said.

"So is this place haunted?" the tall one with a touch of premature gray at his temples asked as if he hadn't really been listening to the rest of the conversation.

I knew that Coventry got its fair share of paranormal investigators because the ley line attracted sensitive people, but I had never heard of a ghost hunting show filming here. I had no idea what the proper protocol was for dealing with them, and I'd just woken up.

"Are you guys planning on doing your show about Coventry?" I asked with a yawn.

"We are, but we're waiting for the courthouse to open so we can get a filming permit," Kurt said.

"Right, and you thought you'd stop and investigate some spooky places or like scout locations or something while you wait," I said.

"Exactly," Grateful Dead said.

"Okay, well, across the street is a very old and historic cemetery. You can't see it from here, but just go over the fence and you'll find it. Go wait over there while I get dressed in something other than my robe and I'll see if I can help you," I said.

"Really, an old cemetery hidden in the woods?" Kurt asked. He rubbed his hands together with glee like a kid on Christmas morning. It was actually a little bit endearing.

"Yep. The oldest part is right on the other side of the fence. If you keep going through the tree line on the other side, there's a much newer section. None of it's used anymore and hasn't been for a long time," I said. "I'll come over there as soon as I can."

I shut the door and started up the stairs to get dressed. Meri appeared at the top of the steps on the landing.

"What are you going to do?" he asked. "You can't let the Ghost Squeakers in here."

"Ghost Seekers," I said as Meri rolled his eyes at me. "I don't know, but I don't feel like I should just leave them wandering around Coventry knocking on doors. So I'll take them to the courthouse. I don't imagine the witches on the town council are going to be too pleased about this."

"You're going to present the Ghost Squeakers to the town council?" Meri asked. "For what? They can't film a show here. We'd be exposed to the whole world. We should tell them we're taking them somewhere haunted and lock them in the Skeenbauer Crypt."

"Meri, we can't lock them in the crypt with the scary dead witches just because they heard Coventry was haunted and want to do their show here. That wouldn't be right," I said as I walked past him to get dressed.

"We could drive lead them to the edge of town and make them forget Coventry exists."

"That would only work until they found whatever information brought them here again," I said from my room as I tugged on my jeans.

"Well, there has to be something. The witches of Coventry can make every human in this town willfully ignore the magic around them. I don't understand why these ghost hunters and paranormal investigators keep showing up here. Now we've got ones that want to film a show."

"The good news is that so far, the magic that keeps the human residents of Coventry ignoring the magic around them works on the visitors too. None of them ever really find anything because they ignore it too."

"Yeah, but these people have cameras and equipment, Brighton," Meri said. "We can't make cameras willfully ignore what's right in front of them."

"We still have to let the council decide," I said.

"No, we don't. The town council is half human, and they aren't going to see a problem with this. The half of the council that are witches will have their hands tied. We can stop this now."

"I don't see a way that we can without possibly hurting innocent people, Meri. We'll do our best to protect the town, but I'm taking them to the council," I said.

"What is going on?" Brody asked.

He stepped out of what was the spare bedroom, but had sort of become his bedroom. My brother ran his hand through his tousled hair and scratched his stomach sleepily.

"How did the pounding on the door not wake you?" I asked.

"It did, but I heard you get up. Figured you'd get the door," he said.

"What if it had been a killer or something?"

"Then you've got Meri here," he said and waved his hand in the cat's direction. "But don't worry, I totally would have come to your aid, big sis."

"I don't need your help anyway," I said with a chuckle. "So there are some ghost hunters in town that do a show called *Ghost Seekers*. That's who was pounding on the door. Anyway, I'm going to take them to the town council. They want a filming permit."

"Ugh, that show is ridiculous," Brody said.

"Let me guess. I've never watched it, but if you don't like it that must mean the historical stuff they present is inaccurate," I said.

"Yeah," Brody agreed.

"Except that everything you know about history is incorrect," I said. "You know that from being here."

"Oh, crap. You're right," Brody said and turned on his heels.

"Where are you going?"

"I have to go binge watch the show again," he said. "If they get the permit to

13

film here, I'll need to speak with them about their sources. What if I've been wrong all along, and the stuff they present is all based on clandestine but accurate sources."

"All right. Call me if you need me," I said as I headed down the stairs.

My stomach rumbled when I got to the bottom. My belly wanted breakfast, but there was no time for such concerns. I didn't want to leave the Ghost Seekers milling around the old graveyard for too long.

"Ahem," Meri said as I put my hand on the front door knob. "You might be willing to ignore your hunger, but I signed up for no such thing."

"Right, sorry," I said. "Let me grab you a quick can of tuna, and then I'm off."

"I'd prefer smoked salmon," Meri said.

"Of course, you would," I countered. "Don't worry, I've got some."

While he ate his salmon, I snarfed down a slice of cheese followed by a spoonful of peanut butter. A big spoonful. It wasn't much, but I knew from experience the combo would hold me for a while. It was my go-to breakfast back in the city when I was late for work.

Once Meri was fed, I headed across the street to the old cemetery. Two of the six Ghost Seekers were in the old part of the graveyard, and I startled them when I arrived. I could only guess that the other three had wandered off to the newer section.

"I'm sorry, I don't think I caught your names," I said to the female crew member and one of the guys who hadn't really said anything when they were all on my porch. There was Kurt, the guy with the camera, Grateful Dead, and the one with a touch of gray hair. And there was this guy.

"Bobby Lucas," he said and stuck out his hand.

"And I'm Rachel Boggs," the woman said as I shook Bobby's hand.

"Sorry, we're not used to interacting with people who have no idea who we are," Bobby said. "We should have done better with our introductions."

"Let's see," Rachel said. "You know Kurt's name. The guy in the Grateful Dead shirt, and he will always be wearing a Grateful Dead shirt, is Link Meyers. It's seriously all he owns. Toto James is our main camera man. Toto is a nickname."

"He's from Kansas?" I guessed.

"Exactly," Rachel said. "None of us know his real name either."

"And Chris Gather is the brain," Bobby said. "The guy with the early gray. Chris is our research assistant and does whatever else we need when he's not knee-deep in online investigation or nose-deep in a book."

"It's nice to meet you," I said. "Even if it was a bit unexpected. So where is the rest of your crew? The courthouse will be opening for the day. We should head that way."

"They are over in the newer part of the cemetery doing EVP readings," Rachel said. "Bobby and I were trying to get some photos of these headstones so Chris could research the names later."

"Why don't you round everyone up and I'll meet you at the front of the courthouse. Unless you don't know where it is and need to follow me?"

"Nope. We saw it on our way in," Rachel said.

"Besides, we have GPS if we didn't," Bobby added.

"Oh, I wouldn't count on your GPS around here," I said. "They don't work well in Coventry."

"Oh," Bobby said with a smile. "Must be that ley line business Chris was talking about. Paranormal interference with our equipment already." He rubbed his hands together. "This is going to be good."

"I don't know about paranormal. More like a run of the mill magnetic anomaly. Nothing supernatural about it," I lied.

"We'll have to see," Rachel said skeptically. "But that's what we're here for."

"Great," I said, not wanting to comment or lie further. "I'll see you at the courthouse then."

I pulled into one of the parking spaces out in front of the courthouse in my car that the Ghost Seekers had assumed was just a broken-down, abandoned vehicle. Their van pulled in close to me a minute later.

There weren't many people around the square at that time of day, but the ones that were rubber-necked at the newcomers. It didn't help that *Ghost Seekers* was painted across both sides of their van in huge red letters that looked as though they were dripping blood.

"Ah. The Skeenbauer and Tuttlesmith statue," Chris said as we walked past it. "The two founding clans. I've read rumors that they are actually witches. Family covens."

"Of course," I said over my shoulder. "A town founded and run by women so they have to be witches. They couldn't possibly have just been strong women."

"I didn't mean anything by it," Chris said quickly.

"Let's just see what the council has to say about a filming permit," was my only answer. "They should all be here, but I'm not sure how long you'll have to wait. They don't assemble for things at the drop of the hat."

"I told you we should have applied for the permit in advance," Rachel said, but I wasn't sure where she'd directed her complaint.

"We've been over this," Kurt said. "We weren't planning on coming here until next season, Rachel."

"You weren't coming to Coventry until your next season?" I asked. "So why did you decide to come early?"

"The last place we were going to go didn't, eh…" Kurt stopped and ran his hand through his hair. "It didn't work out."

"Something you guys did?"

"No. I mean, we never even went there. It happened the day before we were supposed to start filming," Toto said. "A place not that far from here. You might have heard of it. Pine Grove? It's an old summer camp. Anyway, there were a bunch of murders there recently. The whole place is off limits for the time being, and we've got a production schedule to stick to."

"Oh," I said. "I've heard of Pine Grove, but I had no idea that happened. That's too bad."

"More ghosts for us when we do get around to filming there," Grateful Dead said.

"Link," Chris chastised. "Don't be like that."

"Sorry, man," Link said sheepishly. "But it's true."

"Let's just go find out about your filming permit," I said.

I detected that a bickering session had been on the horizon, and even though I really didn't have anything better to do, I didn't want to spend my time listening to the Ghost Seekers have it out in front of the courthouse. My plan worked, though, and they followed me inside silently. No doubt taking in their surroundings. I was just glad the specter that frequently appeared to me in the top floor window had been a no-show that day.

Hopefully it stayed that way when I took the group up to the top floor to speak with the members of the council. Everyone stepped onto the elevator except Bobby.

"I'll wait for the next one," he said. "Top floor, right?"

"I'll wait with you," Rachel said, but her voice was tinged with annoyance. I could have sworn she rolled her eyes too.

"Yeah. Top floor," I said. "But come right up. I don't want you to get caught wandering around the courthouse unescorted."

"Don't worry," Bobby said. "I'm not trying to sneak around and investigate this building. Though I would love to investigate it."

"He just doesn't like enclosed spaces," Rachel added.

"All right," I said and punched the button for the top floor. "See you guys at the top."

As soon as the elevator doors closed, I got a bad feeling. I'm not sure what it was about, but the only thing I could think of was that the elevator would open and that hideous specter that was always watching me from the top floor would be there waiting.

Thankfully, it wasn't. Well, it wasn't right outside the doors.

"What was that?" Toto asked as he stepped into the hall.

It was a good thing that he didn't have his camera. By the time any of them pulled their phones out and started recording, the thing with the pale skin and black holes for eyes had disappeared into one of the councilmen's offices.

"I think that was Betty? I think her name is Betty. She's a secretary for a couple of the council members," I said too quickly.

"That was no secretary," Kurt said. "That thing had black eyes."

"Betty has been having some health issues," I said. "I sincerely hope if we encounter her again, you're a little more empathetic."

Kurt just stared at me with his mouth hanging open for a moment. I knew I was lying, and I got the feeling he knew I was lying, but I'd left him in a position where he couldn't say anything more without coming off like a jerk. He probably didn't want me putting in a bad word about them with the council, so Kurt dropped it.

I wasn't exactly sure how to get a filming permit in Coventry, and I wished I'd gone down to the archives to ask Remy first. But I was glad I'd decided not to take Ghost Seekers down there. The last thing Remy needed was to have to deal with these guys nosing around in his archives.

I thought it would be a good idea to take the question of the filming permit to one of the council members who was a witch first. "You guys wait out here," I said to the Ghost Seekers once Bobby and Rachel had joined us. "I'm going to go talk to Councilwoman Hanks."

I went into Melissa Hanks' office and closed the door behind myself. Melissa's secretary wasn't at her desk. Probably because she shared a secretary with other members of the council. They all shared the same few secretaries.

Someone was moving around in Melissa's office, so I walked up and knocked gently on the door that separated the public portion of the office from Melissa's private office space.

"Yes?" Melissa called through the door. "Patty, is that you?"

"No, it's Brighton," I said. "Brighton Longfield. I need to talk to you."

"Come in."

I went into her office and closed the door behind me. Melissa was a Skeenbauer witch who had married a human, much to the Skeenbauer family dismay, but she'd also worked her way onto the Coventry Town Council. I figured that of the council members, she was the best one to bring the problem to initially.

"I'm sorry to bother you without making an appointment," I said as I took a seat in the chair across from her desk. "But we have sort of a situation."

"Really? What's wrong?"

"Okay, so have you heard of the show *Ghost Seekers*?"

"Oh, no," she said and rubbed her temples. "I already know I'm not going to like where this is going, but we witches all knew it was only a matter of time before one of those shows came to Coventry. So what is it? Is there a buzz on the net that they want to come here? Are they advertising a trip to Coventry in their commercials?"

"They're out in the hall. Their last location had a huge delay, so now they're here to apply for a film permit."

"What? Wait, did you know they were coming?" Melissa asked.

"I didn't. I had no idea who they were until they showed up on my front porch this morning. They were hoping Hangman's House was abandoned."

"This isn't going to go over well," she said and rubbed her temples again. "Thank you, Brighton. I'll take it from here."

Chapter Two

I was a little surprised when Thorn showed up at my house after his shift. I don't know why, but I hadn't expected to see him. Fortunately, Brody and I had ordered pizza, and we had more than enough to share.

"All we've got is a large cheese and a large pepperoni," I said. "We weren't expecting you, but I'm more than happy to share."

"Are you sure?"

"Yes, of course I'm sure. Come in. I'm happy to see you."

I kissed him, and sadly, I was actually surprised when he didn't pull back. Things between us had become strained so fast that it almost made my head spin.

"I'm happy to see you too," Thorn said and pulled me into his arms.

I listened to his heart beat for a few seconds while we stood there. It wasn't a comforting sound. His pulse was too fast, and it seemed clunky.

"You're not all right," I said as our embrace broke.

"We need to talk about what's going on," Thorn said. "I want to clear the air about all of this, but I don't want to discuss it in front of your brother. Okay?"

"Sure," I said. "He took some pizza up to his room a while ago. He's binge watching that *Ghost Seekers* show. I don't imagine he'll be down anytime soon."

"Them. About that," Thorn said and rubbed the back of his neck. "Those guys are a pain in the butt."

"Why?"

"I got calls about them all day. People have no idea who they are or what they're doing here, so they keep calling dispatch. I imagine it's only going to get worse tonight."

"Well, then I guess you better get some pizza while you have the chance. There's Pepsi in the fridge too," I said.

I had planned on eating some pizza too, but Thorn saying we needed to talk had tied me up in knots. Instead, I grabbed a diet soda from the fridge and joined him at the kitchen table.

"You're not going to eat?" he asked.

"I will in a bit," I said. "You said we needed to talk?"

"I didn't mean to make you worry. In fact, that's why I came here. I figured that if you knew what was going on, you'd worry less," Thorn said. "You already know that my ex-wife is in town, and that she brought a little girl with her. Brighton, the little girl is my daughter."

"And she kept it from you all this time? She never told you she had your baby?"

"Sadie thought the baby was my brother's child," Thorn said with a sigh.

"What?"

"My ex-wife started a relationship with my brother right after we split up. I mean, the whole thing started before we split up, but they didn't get together officially until after the split."

"How did you not know about any of this?" I asked.

"Because my brother and I are mostly estranged. He had no problems having a relationship with my wife, so it should be pretty obvious why."

"So how do you know the kid isn't his?"

"Eventually, Todd got tired of playing house with Sadie and Dani. That's the little girl, my daughter's, name. He suspected that there was a chance that Dani was mine, so he demanded a DNA test. Which he got through a court order. He wanted to ditch them and move onto something else, but Todd didn't want to be forced to pay child support. He was right, and the test proved that Dani wasn't his, but it also proved that it was a close genetic relationship. I've seen the test results, Brighton. Dani is mine. It's why Sadie ran off and never came back. It's why she would call me to talk even after we split, but I never saw her. She didn't want me to know, but she knew that I wouldn't just let the relationship go if I knew she was pregnant. I would have fought for our marriage, but Sadie didn't want that. She wanted Todd."

"So now what?" I asked a little more bluntly than I intended.

I couldn't help it. All of his talk about not letting the marriage go when he knew his child was involved was exactly what I was afraid of from the moment he told me.

"That depends on you," Thorn said. "I love you, but we've never had a discussion about kids. I have no idea if you'd ever even wanted them, and we couldn't have possibly talked about how you felt about being a stepmother."

"Stepmother?" The word wasn't as scary as I'd thought.

"Yeah. I'm sorry if this all seems quick. We weren't talking about marriage yet, so thrusting things like the word stepmother on you seems unfair. But, Brighton, I don't know what else to do. I wouldn't feel right proceeding with our relationship unless you thought that you might be okay with a child at some point."

"And you're not at all worried that talking about marriage and me helping you raise Dani is too fast?" The question was a delay so I could wrap my head around what was happening.

"I mean, I guess I assumed that marriage was where we were headed. Maybe not tomorrow, but someday. Right?"

"Yes, of course that's where I thought we were heading, but I wasn't sure anymore after you told me that. I assumed you've been gone because you've been spending time with your ex-wife. I thought that perhaps you were considering reconciling with her so you could be a family with your daughter."

"Sadie's and my romantic relationship is over," Thorn said. "Any time I've been spending with her was only so that we could figure out how to co-parent Dani. That's it."

"That's good to hear," I said. "So what does this mean for us in the immediate future?"

Thorn was just about to answer when he got a call from dispatch. Sure enough, someone had called in a report about the Ghost Seekers poking around an abandoned house. They had their filming permit and weren't technically trespassing, but Thorn had to leave anyway to go smooth the situation over.

"I'll call you soon," he said and kissed my cheek. "Thanks for the pizza."

As soon as he was gone, I noticed that I still felt completely unsettled. His words should have made me feel better than they did, but I still felt like something was amiss.

Seconds later, my phone rang. "So word around town is your new friends, the Ghost Seekers, are poking around the old abandoned Grant House," Remy said as soon as I answered.

"Yeah, Thorn's on his way over there to smooth things over."

"When he's gone, you want to go see what they're up to?" Remy seemed enthusiastic.

"You think they'll stick around after Thorn talks to them?"

"Oh, yeah. They've got their film permit and the Grant House technically belongs to Coventry since it's been abandoned for so long. They've dealt with law enforcement far meaner than Thorn in the course of their show."

"I guess maybe we should," I said.

"If nothing else, we can make sure that they don't find anything to upload to YouTube tonight," Remy said.

"YouTube?"

"Oh, you didn't know? They have a web series now that coincides with their television show. They post outtakes, raw footage, and teasers when they think they've got something."

"That sounds like it could be a disaster," I said.

"It does. So we should do our civic duty and go assist them," Remy said. "Plus, it will cheer you up. I know you're down. I can feel it."

"So should I meet you there?"

"Nah, I'll come pick you up. Give me ten to fifteen minutes."

"No rush," I said. "We want to make sure Thorn's gone before we show up anyway."

I could tell Remy wanted to ask me if there was more to my statement than just the issue with the ghost hunting crew, but he didn't. I didn't volunteer the information either.

When I went upstairs to tell Brody that I was leaving with Remy, his bedroom door was wide open. He was on the bed on his stomach watching the *Ghost Seekers* episodes with his headphones in. I tried knocking on the door frame before I went in, but he didn't hear me. I thought about walking up behind him and tapping his shoulder, but I figured that would scare him. Instead, I walked around and stood in front of him.

Brody hit the space bar and paused his video. "What's up?" he asked without taking the earbuds out.

"Remy and I are going out. The Ghost Seekers are over at a place called the Grant House, we're going to go keep an eye on things," I said. "You want to come?"

"Nah. I'll leave the field work to my betters. I'll be here doing research."

Ten minutes later, Remy pulled up in the driveway. I was sitting out on the front steps waiting for him when he arrived. He started to get out of the car, but I put my hand up to stop him.

Once I slid into the passenger seat and clicked my seatbelt, we were off. "I almost can't believe the council gave them a filming permit," I said after a few moments of silence.

"The witches didn't want to, but they couldn't think of a good reason not to do it. Denying them the permit would have just looked even more suspicious," Remy said.

"You'd think they could have come up with something. The council could have told them there was a six-month waiting period or something. If they'd delayed it, the Ghost Seekers would have had to wander off and find something else," I said.

"You should be on the council," Remy said with a smile.

"No thanks." I retorted and poked him in the arm.

"Well, the humans on the town council have no idea why this is a terrible idea, and the witches are hoping that the magic that keeps the human townsfolk looking in the other direction will work on the Ghost Seekers too."

"But we both know that's too big of a risk, and that's why we're on our way to Grant House, right?"

"That and I wanted the opportunity to hang out with you again. Like we used to when you were restoring the old cemetery."

"Well, it won't be like that because the Ghost Seekers will be there too," I said.

"But we'll be a team again," he said hopefully.

"We never were not a team," I said. "We had some struggles, but we were never not a team."

"Sometimes it felt like you hated me," he said.

"And sometimes it felt like you really didn't like me either, but it wasn't real," I said. "Misunderstandings and misplaced feelings were all it was."

"I'm sorry that I got mad at you because Annika figured out that Langoria was my mother. I never should have assumed the worst about you," he said as he turned down the street for Grant House. "And I never should have been spying on you."

"What happened?" I asked as we pulled up behind the Ghost Seeker van. "I mean, why were you doing that? It's so unlike you. You're not a stalker, Remy."

"The night that I came to your house and told you that Thorn would break your heart, I was wrong. I mean that I was wrong to do that. I knew as soon as I had that I had screwed up, so I used that magic on you to make it seem like a dream. But you're too strong for that. You knew it was real, but that's not the point. I shouldn't have done that. Using my magic for personal gain should have had consequences, but I did another spell to try and negate those. It was one stupid mistake after another."

"But that doesn't explain why you were outside my house watching Thorn and me."

"It does," he said with a sigh. "Because of my actions, I let darkness in. I had a bad spirit attached to me. It tormented me day and night. The Aunties wouldn't help get rid of it. They forbid Annika from getting rid of it."

"You should have come to me. I would have helped you."

"I know you would have, but I was afraid it would hurt you. Then, it started telling me that it was hurting you. It told me that Thorn was hurting you too. Not just your heart. I know it sounds stupid, but that thing had me believing that something bad was going to happen to you. I couldn't sleep. I couldn't eat. My thoughts just got darker and darker. It said you betrayed me, and that you had to pay. I don't know. Everything got foggy after that, but as you know, I eventually managed to pull myself out of it all."

"I mean it, Remy, you should have come to me. I thought you were watching me because you were jealous of Thorn's and my relationship. I had no idea," I said.

"I think we'll be all right."

"I know we will. Well, we'll be okay as long as we keep these chuckle butts from exposing all of Coventry's secrets. Brody is watching all of their old shows, but do you know if they've ever actually caught anything? Do they have any real footage of ghosts?"

"There's some stuff that could be real, but it's nothing definitive. I'm less worried about them catching ghosts and more worried about them getting a witch using magic," Remy said.

When I looked up, Chris was standing on the sidewalk near Remy's car watching us. He saw me looking and offered a small wave.

"Well, let's do it then," I said.

"Brighton, good evening," Chris said as I emerged from the car.

"Hello, Chris."

"What brings you out?" he asked as Remy joined us on the sidewalk.

"This is my friend Remy. He works in the town archives. We thought we'd come out and check out what you're doing," I said.

"We're just doing a light investigation around the perimeter of the house. The sheriff was just here, but he left pretty quickly after getting a call from his wife about his daughter."

"Ex-wife." I grumbled.

"What?" Chris was genuinely perplexed as he had no idea what was going on between Thorn and me.

"Oh, nothing."

Sensing that it was a topic he didn't want to be involved in, Chris turned his attention to Remy. "So you work in the town archives? That must be amazing."

"It's pretty cool," Remy said with a smile. "So why are you guys only doing the perimeter of the house?"

"Well, we knew the house was abandoned, but we didn't want to get arrested for trespassing so soon."

"It wouldn't be trespassing," Remy said. "The house is technically public property. You could go in as long as you don't do any harm."

"Remy?" I couldn't believe he was encouraging that.

"It's true, Brighton. I would know. I've got all the records on this place stored in the archives."

"Do you think I might be able to get a look at those?" Chris asked. "This place's history is fascinating."

"Sure, during regular business hours, of course. You should come by tomorrow. I can show you what I've got."

"For now, can I ask you some questions?"

"I'm just going to go look for the rest of the crew," I said when I sensed that they were about to have a long, boring talk about historical documents.

Brody should have come along. I'd make sure to let him know about Chris and Remy meeting at the archives the next day. He'd definitely want to be there for that.

"Could you let the others know they can go inside if the doors are unlocked?" Chris asked.

"Sure thing."

No one else was in the front of the house, so I walked around to the side. The backyard was surrounded by a crumbling privacy fence, but the gate was open. I didn't have to risk ripping it off its rusty hinges just to gain access to the yard.

The other Ghost Seekers were in the back milling around. Kurt looked as though he was practicing lines, and Toto was filming the whole thing. Link sat along the back fence in the lotus pose with his eyes closed. I figured he might have been trying to contact a spirit, and I wondered if he knew how much he probably didn't want that to happen.

Rachel was off in another corner with an EMF reader in one hand and a small recorder in the other. I didn't know much about ghost hunting, but I did know she was trying to get EVP readings.

I didn't need the EMF reader to know that there was a mischievous spirit nearby. It wasn't making itself visible, but I could feel it. She was going to get something on the electronic voice phenomenon readings.

Well, she was going to get something until I came along.

A little wave of my hand and her recording would be nothing convincing. I felt the spirit that had been trying to communicate with her rush past me in a cold breeze. Most likely it wasn't happy with me, but I didn't care. At least it hadn't fully manifested and started throwing chunks of rotten fence at us.

"Oh, hey," Kurt said when he saw me watching the scene. "Did you just come to check out what we're doing? Because if you want to be on the show, we'll need you to sign a waiver."

"I thought I'd come see how you guys were doing. You don't want me on the show."

"Why not?" Kurt said as he crossed the yard to me. "You've definitely got the face for television."

"Don't let Rachel hear you say that." Bobby stepped out from behind a huge tree in the yard. I hadn't noticed him back there, and I'd kind of forgotten about him until that moment. He definitely had that blending into the background thing down.

"I already did hear him," Rachel said without joining us.

"Yeah, she heard me," Kurt said with a chuckle. "Good thing she's not the jealous type."

"Not even a little bit." Rachel looked over and gave me a warm smile that time. "Besides, he's right. She does have a face meant for television."

"You guys," I said, but I wasn't sure what to say. I didn't want to be one of those people who couldn't take a compliment, but I did have a hard time with compliments. So I changed the subject. "Chris and my friend Remy are talking out front. Remy wanted you guys to know that Grant House here is public property, so as long as you don't damage anything, you can go inside."

"Is it unlocked?" Kurt asked.

"I don't know. Probably," I said with a shrug. "It's a small town. And since you've had a visit from the sheriff already, several in fact, you know how close an eye people from Coventry keep on their surroundings."

"You don't think the neighbors will call the sheriff again if they see us going in?" Bobby asked.

By then Link and Rachel had joined us. They were all watching me expectantly.

"He's my boyfriend," I said. "I'll send him a text letting him know you're going in and it's perfectly legal."

"All right, all right!" Bobby exclaimed. "We're in business. I'm going to go try the door."

As I expected, the back door was unlocked. I followed the Ghost Seekers inside, and as I also expected, there was no power.

"Let's get some lights set up in here. Something dim. I want it to mimic candlelight ambiance," Kurt said as we all stood gathered in the kitchen.

"On it, boss," Link said. "I'll get some lighting from the van."

"You want to stick around and see how it's done?" Kurt asked.

"Sure," I said. "I haven't watched any ghost hunting shows, though. So I'm afraid I don't have any frame of reference."

"That's okay. Your first will be the best," Bobby said. "Kurt stays in front of the camera most of the time, but I'll hang back with you and fill you in on what's going on."

"You're not going to do the EMF reader or EVP with me?" Rachel asked.

"Not this round," Bobby said. "The rooms in this old Victorian are too narrow for us to crowd together. Since I'll be hanging with Brighton for this investigation, I'll shoot some still photos."

"K," Rachel said.

"One thing I like to do is just shoot a flash camera into dark rooms. Sometimes we get some inexplicable things that way,"

Bobby said when he turned his attention back to me.

"Most of the time we just get orbs," Toto said.

"Orbs are a sign of the paranormal, though," I said.

"Yeah, they are," Toto responded. "Unless they are caused by a camera flash off of hardwood floors or wall coverings."

"We still occasionally get something," Bobby retorted.

"He's right. We do," Rachel said more to me than anyone else.

Link came back into the house and started to set up the lighting with Toto's and Rachel's help. Bobby stuck close to me.

"So what do you know about the history of Grant House?" Bobby asked while everyone else was busy.

"Not much. I'm actually kind of new to Coventry myself," I said.

"Do you want to know?" Bobby asked. "Do you want to know why we chose this place?"

"I thought you chose it because it was abandoned. Same reason you tried to get into Hangman's House."

"We're still working on the history of Hangman's House, but Grant House we know a lot about. I can't believe you live in a town like Coventry and you aren't interested in this stuff," he said.

"You should tell me why you're interested," I said with a shrug.

"Cool. So it's called the Grant House because it was built by William Grant back in the late 1800s as a gift for his second wife. His first wife had died under mysterious circumstances in New York State, and the rumors that his second wife had poisoned her followed them here. Some people said that the second Mrs. Grant was a distant relative to the Skeenbauer clan, and that's why they weren't run out of town.

"Mr. and Mrs. Grant had to rent a house while this one was built. Originally, they intended to stay at the local inn, but the construction of Grant House took far longer than expected. A couple of laborers died on the job, and others complained of the specter of an angry woman tormenting and even hurting them while they tried to work. Mr. and Mrs. Grant insisted that the two workers who died here were drunk on the job, and they denied the rumors that the ghost was that of the first Mrs. Grant back from the grave to exact revenge on her husband, his much younger second wife, and anyone who helped them."

"That's pretty creepy," I said. "But it seems like that all happened a long time ago. Why would the house be abandoned now?"

"If our research is correct, it's been abandoned since around the 1970s. Before it was abandoned, it was owned by a string of people. None of the owners ever lived in the house very long. They would move out and try to rent the house out. No tenant would ever stay long, though. That went on for about fifty years. From the 1920s until the 1970s. Someone would buy the house thinking they were getting an extraordinary deal. They'd move out a short time later. Try to rent the house several times, and then put it back on the market for the next person to buy."

"But that all stopped in the seventies?"

"The last owner lived in the house for three days," Bobby said. "His accounts of what he saw in the house during that time led him to specifically make a will that left the house to the town of Coventry. He refused to rent it out, and he didn't want anyone else living here."

"So he's not alive then and we can't talk to him," I said.

"Oh, no. That's the thing. He came back here one last time twenty years after he abandoned the place and made the will. He came back here and took his own life in one of the upstairs bedrooms."

"How do you know all of this?"

"His story is public record, Brighton. The man's name was Gregory Peck. He left accounts of what he saw and instructions to make it all public with his lawyer."

"So what did he see?" I asked.

"You sure you want to know?" Bobby asked. "We can wait until we're not in the house anymore."

"I'm not afraid," I said.

"All right,," Bobby said. "The story goes that Peck moved into the house in the middle of summer. Back then, people didn't have air conditioning, so they had open windows and box fans instead.

"Peck had all of the downstairs windows open, but he only had a fan for two windows. The one in the living room was in the side window because there was a breeze coming from that direction. The front window was open to the street, but had no fan.

"He was unpacking boxes when he heard a strange sound from the front of the house."

"What kind of strange sound?" I asked.

"At first he thought it was a rustling in the bushes under the window. Thinking it was a racoon or something, Peck ignored the sound at first. The noise grew louder, and Peck turned off the living room fan so he could get a better listen.

"It was then that he realized the sound wasn't a rustling, but instead was scratching noises. He said that the sound made his blood run cold for reasons he couldn't quite put his finger on. When he rushed over to shut the window, someone knocked on the door.

"Peck went to the door and opened it to find no one there. As he was closing the door and locking it, the scratching at the window started again. Only it was scraping the glass since he'd closed and locked the window.

"He got a hold of himself and shook off his thoughts of something sinister. Peck decided it was kids playing a prank, and went outside to run them off. When he went outside, he confirmed that no one was out there. The problem was that the front door slammed behind him.

"Peck looked inside the house through the front window and saw a black figure standing in his living room. He didn't go back into the house that night, but instead checked into a motel. Peck waited until late morning to go back the next day. He checked to see if anything was stolen just in case what he saw in the house was a burglar. As he suspected, nothing was missing, but there were scratch marks on the floor outside of the bedroom he'd planned to use as his own.

"It was enough to freak him out, but Peck had just purchased the house. He didn't want to give up on it. The idea of walking away from such a large purchase didn't sit right with him. He convinced himself that the scratches could have been there all along and he just hadn't noticed them because of the lighting or perhaps a rug in the hall. Peck further convinced himself that the dark figure he saw in the living room could have just been his own reflection, and the noise caused by an animal after all."

"I'm guessing his excuses were wrong?" I asked.

"Yes, but at first he thought he was right. Nothing scary happened that afternoon while he unpacked his boxes and cleaned. A neighbor even came over with cookies and didn't say anything about the house being haunted. Peck didn't ask, but he took the neighbor's visit as a good sign.

"That evening he made himself some dinner and watched television before going to bed. Peck was happy that he hadn't abandoned the house, and he chalked the previous evening's events off to nerves. While purchasing the house hadn't been an unpleasant experience, he was buying a house for unpleasant reasons. Greg Peck had just gone through a divorce, and he thought that perhaps he was just still feeling the effects from that.

"Peck turned in for the evening and had an easy time going to sleep because he'd had a couple of beers while watching television. Convinced that nothing was spooky about the house and buzzed from the beer, he felt completely relaxed.

"In the middle of the night, he found out how wrong he'd been to come back to the house. When he awoke, Peck thought that a strong breeze was blowing the blanket and tickling his toe. When he come to all the way, Peck realized that his bedroom window was closed. But something was pulling on his foot.

"Seconds later, he was yanked onto the floor. He jumped up and looked around, but he was alone. Peck walked down the hall looking for some explanation for what was happening to him. He smelled sulfur and then the air around him turned ice cold before he was knocked to the floor."

"A demon," I said.

"Oh, so you do believe in this stuff," Bobby said.

"I've seen movies," I retorted.

"Okay," Bobby said, but I could tell he didn't entirely believe me. "Anyway, yeah.

Peck believed that the thing that confronted him in the house was a demon. He grabbed his wallet from the nightstand and headed downstairs to the living room. There he met the dark figure he'd seen from the night before. Only it wasn't just a shadow anymore. He wrote that it wasn't really a solid figure either. The stench of sulfur was almost overpowering, and Peck said that the creature's eyes felt like they were burning his skin. He only looked into them for a moment, but when he did, he felt like he was dying. In fact, later in life, he wrote that he saw him hang himself in the upstairs bedroom."

"That could have been self-fulfilling prophesy," I said.

"But the rest of it?" Bobby asked.

"I don't know," I said. "Why did he and his wife get divorced? Was it possible that he had some sort of profound mental illness? What about the differences in the stories?"

"What do you mean?"

"I mean that the first story is about a ghost, and the one about Gregory Peck is about a demon," I answered.

"Hey, guys, come up here," Kurt called out.

It sounded like he was upstairs. I hadn't noticed that everyone but Bobby and I had gone upstairs.

"What is it?" Bobby yelled.

"There's a definite cold spot up here. Rachel's getting off-the-charts EMF readings too."

"Let's go," Bobby said.

As soon as we got upstairs, I could tell the spirit was the same one that was outside in the yard. Other than the cold spot and the EMF reading, it didn't manifest further.

But a loud knocking sound emanated from downstairs. It startled all of us even though everyone but me was supposed to be seasoned ghost hunters.

"Let's go see what that was," Kurt said. He patted my arm on the way by. "You're good luck."

"I'm going to stay up here and keep taking readings," Rachel said.

"I'll help her up here," Link said and got out his phone. "I can get secondary footage with my phone if we need it."

I shot off a text to Remy as we all made our way back down the creaky stairs of the old house. *We've got activity in here. You should come inside now.*

As soon as we were all down the stairs and trying to spread out in the living room area, a scratching started outside the front window. The exact thing that had happened in the story Bobby told me.

My first instinct was to panic, but a thought occurred to me before terror could take hold. What if it was a spirit that overheard Bobby telling me the history of Grant House, and it was just trying to scare us? Still, I wished I'd brought Meri along in case it was a horrible demon. He had his way of putting them in their place like no one else.

The next round of scratching began just as Remy walked in the door. He stopped halfway in and then stuck his head out the door to look at the outside of the front window.

"Do you see anything?" I asked.

"Not a thing," he said, and the scratching stopped.

Remy had taken the wind out of the spirit's game. The Ghost Seekers just sort of looked at each other, murmured somethings, and then broke apart to continue their investigation. Bobby, who had volunteered to stay at my side, eventually drifted upstairs to where Link and Rachel were investigating. I actually ended up playing some cupcake game on my phone for a couple of hours until the Ghost Seeker crew decided to break out sleeping bags and spend the night.

In my opinion, I decided that was outside of my civic duty and had Remy take me home, after we put a few quick warding spells on the house on the way out. The Ghost Seekers weren't going to see anything more that night, and if they did, the wards would erase the footage when they left the house.

It probably wasn't the nicest thing, but I didn't want to stay there babysitting them. I wanted my bed.

Chapter Three

The next morning, I awoke to my phone ringing. I reached over to the nightstand and knocked it to the floor. That hadn't been my intention, but my hand was asleep. My fingers just swiped at the device like a dead fish, but fortunately, the phone hit the thick rug that stuck out from under my bed and did not break.

Not wanting to actually get out of bed, I just sort of bent at the waist and tried to retrieve the phone without actually getting up. That left me in a state where I was hanging precariously halfway out of the bed. I had to either hoist myself back up using my good arm or just slide the rest of the way off the bed and try not to fall on my face.

As I was deciding, the phone that had gone silent began to ring again. "Yeah. Yeah," I said to no one as I flipped it over to see who was disrupting my morning. It was Remy, and I knew that if he was repeatedly calling, I needed to answer.

Since I hadn't decided how to get myself out of my predicament, I answered the call while hanging from the bed.

"Good morning, Remy." I tried not to sound like I was upside down with all of the blood rushing to my brain.

"Good morning, Brighton. I have bad news."

"Oh, what's that?" I asked as I attempted to push myself back up.

The pins and needles returning to my hand almost landed me on my face, but I recovered. Before Remy answered, I was able to thrust myself up and onto the bed.

"You all right?" Remy asked.

"Yep, I'd just dropped the phone before. Anyway, what's the bad news?"

"The town council would like to see you immediately," he said.

"For what?"

"They didn't tell me specifically, but word is they want to talk to you about our outing last night with the Ghost Seekers."

"Did they talk to you about it?" I asked.

"Nope."

"Then how bad could it be?"

"Just get down here and go to Melissa Hanks' office. She's acting as the spokesperson for the council on this."

"Oh, so I don't have to appear in front of all of them or anything?"

"Nothing like that."

"Great," I said and rubbed my eyes with the back of my hand. "Can you get a message to Melissa that I'll be there in a half hour? I just need some time to get dressed and get coffee."

"Will do."

"I could still make them go away," Meri said when I hung up the phone.

"I don't even want to know what you're thinking," I said. "Come on. Let's get some breakfast, and then I need to get going."

After throwing on some clothes, I trudged down to the kitchen and fed Meri. I didn't want to keep the council waiting, so I skipped food in favor of a big to-go cup filled with iced coffee and lots of hazelnut creamer. Okay, I did take the time for two big spoonfuls of peanut butter too. Meri glanced over his shoulder judgmentally twice in between bites of smoked salmon, but I didn't care. It was good.

"Please work," I said as I slid into the driver's seat of my car.

It had been slightly less than reliable, but I couldn't help but feel like it only broke down for a reason. The car had become like the house. It manipulated my life, and I hoped it was only for my own good.

Fortunately, the car wanted me to make it to my meeting with the council and it started right away. In the time it took me to drive to the courthouse, I downed the whole iced coffee. It just went down so easily.

Up in the top window of the courthouse was my favorite terrifying specter staring down at me. No one was around, and I was hopped up on caffeine, so I waved to it. I made my way inside the building, and as the elevator doors closed, I realized that waving at that hideous ghost might have been a terrible idea.

I held my breath all the way up, but as the doors opened on the top floor, it wasn't there. The secretary was in Melissa's office when I went in. She gave me a look I couldn't quite read and nodded her head toward the inner office door.

"Go on in. She's expecting you."

"Thanks," I said.

I knocked and waited for Melissa's "Come in," before proceeding inside.

Her face wasn't a mask of fury, so I took that as a good sign. "Remy called this morning and said the council wanted to see me," I said as I took the same seat I'd taken the day before.

"We did indeed," Melissa said as she steepled her long, slender fingers. "We have a job for you."

I stared at her with my mouth halfway open for a second. Her crystal blue eyes were cheerful and not a hint of anger resided on her pale porcelain skin.

"You have a job for me? Remy said that this meeting was about us tagging along on the Ghost Seekers' investigation last night. He said that was just gossip, though. Perhaps he was wrong," I rambled.

"No, he was right. It is about that, and it's about a job," she said and brushed one of her dark ringlets away from her face.

"I don't understand."

"The Ghost Seekers were given a filming permit because the witches on the council were afraid that denying it would be too suspicious, but as you've no doubt heard, their presence has caused some issues with the locals. Coventry's citizens are private people, Brighton. Even the humans don't like having a film crew traipsing around town, and they are showing their wariness and displeasure by calling county dispatch way too often. Pretty soon, it's going to get out that we can't handle law enforcement in our little town. Plus, Thorn has a job to do that doesn't involve babysitting a bunch of paranormal investigators."

"He does," I said with an affirmative nod.

"But as far as I know, you don't," she said and smiled. "So you're going to babysit them."

"What?"

"You're going to act as the Ghost Seekers' official escort while they are in Coventry. You'll not only make sure that they don't catch any evidence that there are real witches living in this town, but you'll act as liaison between them and the townsfolk. Just keep the busybodies from calling the police, okay?"

"What about their show? They're here to catch evidence of ghosts and around here, the Ghost Seekers will probably get some pretty convincing stuff," I said.

"Make sure nothing they get is too convincing on the ghost front, but that is secondary to protecting the witches. The Skeenbauers have even agreed to support you since the council has ruled that they can't just turn the visitors into goats."

"All right," I said because I wasn't sure what else to say.

She said they had a job for me, but nothing Melissa had said after that point made it sound like the council was asking. I got the feeling that saying no wasn't an option. If the Skeenbauers were on board, no doubt so that they didn't have to handle the dirty work themselves, that meant I'd have a target on my back even worse than before if I said no.

"Does the job pay anything?"

"Three thousand dollars with a two-thousand-dollar bonus if you can get them to leave town within a week without turning them into goats," she said.

"Meri had some ideas about that," I smirked.

"I can imagine," Melissa's retort came with a hearty laugh. "None of his ideas will work either."

"You haven't even heard them," I said.

"I don't need to hear them, Brighton. Meri is a good familiar under your watchful eye. Let's keep it that way."

"Will I be getting a check from the council this time?"

"The money has already been deposited in your bank account."

"Wow, I mean, I assumed I didn't have a choice in taking this job, but I guess I really didn't have a choice."

"You didn't," Melissa said with a sigh. "You can thank Amelda for that, but I think she's warming up to you. She's trusting you with this, and that's a big deal."

"That's because she knows if I screw it up, she can just banish me. And if I won't go, she can turn me into a bat or have me committed."

"Keep your head down for now, Brighton. Keep impressing the town and this council. The next generation of Skeenbauer witches has a lot more reverence for you than the older generation. Plus, you're a Tuttlesmith. Someday you could be..." Melissa cut off her sentence and cast her eyes down. "Anyway, do a good job for the council, and we'll make sure that you're always taken care of in Coventry."

"Wait, no. You were saying something about me being a Tuttlesmith and I could be... what? I could be what?"

"Nothing that I can talk to you about right now. Please." Her tone was such that I just dropped it.

Coventry and the witch clans that ruled it had their secrets. I just had to be patient, and eventually I'd know all I needed. But that meant I needed to get out there and do the job the council had hired me to do.

Two days into the Ghost Seeker babysitting job and not much had happened. The crew was getting bored, and it seemed like even the ghosts were getting bored. Nothing even close to what had happened the first night happened again, and that included the last night that we'd spent in the cemetery near the Skeenbauer Mausoleum.

I shuddered thinking of the Black Widow Skeenbauer witch inside of the crypt, but I couldn't say anything to Kurt or the other investigators.

Fortunately, Remy had not left me hanging that night. I couldn't sleep, but at least I had him by my side to make me feel a little less vulnerable. A deputy cruiser drove by once in the middle of the night, but it didn't stop. If it was Thorn, he didn't even roll down the window and wave. So, I assumed it was one of the other deputies.

On the morning of the night after we spent in the graveyard, Annika showed up bright and early with hot coffee from Bubble &

Brew. She slipped Remy and me a couple of scones too.

"Sorry, I didn't want to buy pastries for everyone, so keep these on the down low," she whispered into my ear.

Annika, Remy, and I went behind another nearby mausoleum and ate our scones while the Ghost Seekers packed up their equipment and loaded the van.

Kurt came over to where we were sitting when they were all done. "We're going to head over to Mother Hattie's and rent a room so we can take showers. I can't go another day without one," he said.

"You're going to rent a room just to take a shower?" I asked before I swallowed the rest of my coffee.

"Yeah, I can't go another day. And even with dry shampoo, my hair is going to look terrible on camera if I don't wash and condition it."

"You're such a girl," Rachel said.

She'd walked up next to him and hip bumped his playfully. Kurt put his arm around her waist, and for the first time, I realized they were a couple.

"Hey, Rach. Come over here and get a listen to this," Bobby called from a few hundred feet away.

"A woman's work is never done," she said and rolled her eyes.

Kurt kissed her on the head before Rachel took off to go listen to whatever Bobby had found on the recording. I was about to join them so that I could hear too, but Kurt stopped me.

"So do you just want me to call you when we're done showering? We're planning on spending some time investigating the courthouse before it closes. Hopefully everyone will shower quickly, and we'll have most of the day."

"You don't need to get a hotel room to take showers," I said. "I've got two full bathrooms at Hangman's House."

The words were out of my mouth before I really had time to think about the implications. I hadn't wanted the Ghost Seekers in my house at all, and there I was inviting them in to hang out and use my showers.

"Really?" Kurt asked hopefully.

I could tell he expected me to take it back. I should have.

"Sure," I said through a smile. "My brother is there, and my cat doesn't like people. If you can steer clear of them, I think it will be fine."

"We can do that," he said. "We'll stop and pick up something to eat and then meet you there."

"I've got plenty of food too." Once again, it slipped out and I wanted to kick myself.

"That would be amazing. Wow, Brighton. You're really great," Kurt said.

"Let's head out," I said. "I'll let my brother know we're coming."

I turned around to rejoin Annika and Remy. The looks on their faces told me they thought I was insane.

"Are you sure that letting them in your house is a good idea?" Annika asked in a tone that told me she didn't think it was a good idea. "And you offered to make them breakfast? Are you thinking of opening a bed and breakfast?"

"We'll help her," Remy said.

Annika and Remy stayed in the living room and kept an eye on any of the Ghost Seekers that weren't in the shower. The investigators didn't know it, but Meri had his eye on them upstairs. He was there to make sure they didn't go into any of the bedrooms. Meri had also used an illusion spell to keep the Ghost Seekers from noticing the pull-down door to the attic.

While they were doing that, I was in the kitchen cooking. I wasn't hungry because of the scone Annika had brought me, but I had a ton of nervous energy. Thorn had been barely contacting me at that point, and I channeled that anxiety into making a feast for my guests.

There was bacon frying in one pan, and in another I made ham and cheese omelets. Before I'd started with that, I found ingredients in the pantry to make drop biscuits. Those were baking.

The Ghost Seekers could put away some food too. Most of them came into the kitchen and ate before their shower, and they returned when they were done for second breakfast. I just kept cooking as they ate up what I'd made. Eventually, I added hash browns and sausage to the menu. After an hour or so, even Remy and Annika filled up plates and ate too.

"You're worrying," Remy said as he sat at the kitchen table. "You've served everyone food twice now, why don't you come sit and eat too."

"I don't know if I can eat," I said, but my stomach growled.

"I think you can eat," Remy said with a smile.

Annika was in the living room talking to Rachel and hoping Brody would come downstairs. He would as soon as he knew Annika was there, and that's why I hadn't told him. Not that I minded them getting together, but it just seemed like he should take it slow.

Rachel was going over some EVP recordings with Annika, and Annika had to pretend like she didn't know anything about the paranormal. What she did know was that my job was to distract the GS from finding real evidence of the paranormal. Annika gave an Oscar-worthy performance pretending she couldn't hear anything or understand what was being said even when it was obvious Rachel had caught an EVP.

After a while, Remy wandered off to find Brody, and I was left alone in the kitchen. Most of the time, I hated doing the dishes, especially when I couldn't use magic to do them, but I still had so much energy that I went ahead and got started on them.

A few minutes later, Kurt joined me in the kitchen. He grabbed the dish towel and started drying without asking.

"You don't have to do that," I said, but I handed him the glass I'd just finished rinsing.

"I know, but I want to," Kurt said. "I was taught growing up that the cook doesn't do the dishes, so this is the very least I can do."

"But you're a guest," I said.

"Yeah, that's why I'll let you keep washing."

"Well, thank you," I said and did a little curtsy.

"My pleasure," Kurt retorted with a smile.

And then disaster unfolded. I started to laugh when I handed him the next glass, and I'm not sure if I dropped it or he did, but it shattered on the floor.

Without thinking, I bent over and tried to pick up the biggest shards. "Dang it."

"Don't," Kurt warned. "Just leave it, I'll get a broom and dustpan."

But it was too late. I miscalculated my grip and sliced the palm of my hand open on one of the shards that didn't even look sharp. It hurt, and I let out a yelp.

"Where are the clean towels?" Kurt asked.

"Drawer next to the stove," I said not quite sure why.

A second later, I knew. He opened the drawer, grabbed a dark, but clean, dishtowel and knelt beside me. He pressed the towel to my hand.

"Maybe you should go get Remy," I said.

I didn't even think about the fact that Remy and Annika couldn't heal me with the Ghost Seekers there. We could wipe their memory, but I was more afraid of the consequences of that than of the cut.

"No, I'm going to get you to the emergency room," he said. "You're going to need stitches and an evaluation to make sure it didn't hit a nerve."

"I'll be all right," I said. "Just let me go up to the bathroom and take a look."

"Nonsense," Kurt said, and as he did, I swooned a little. "I'm taking you to the hospital now."

"What's going on?" Annika asked as she, Remy, and Brody appeared in the kitchen doorway.

"She needs to get to the hospital," Kurt said.

I wavered on my feet, and Kurt wrapped his arm around my waist and held me up. "I'll be okay. Please just let me go to the bathroom and wash it."

"Let us take her to the bathroom," Remy said.

He knew that the only way they could heal me was to get me away from the others. Instead of relenting, Kurt turned us toward the back door.

"You guys, she needs to go to the hospital," he said. "Hand lacerations aren't something to mess around with. If there's nerve damage, she could lose use of her hand. Waiting is stupid. She has to go now."

Kurt continued to walk me to the back door, and I wasn't sure what to do. My hand hurt badly, and my head was fuzzy. I couldn't see any way to stop Kurt without having to do something to hurt them.

"All right. I'll go," I said.

"I'll drive her," Remy offered.

"I've got this. She can ride in the back of the van. It's easy to wipe down," Kurt said as he walked through the back door.

"Fine, but I'm riding with you," Remy said.

As soon as we were out the back door, I got a bad feeling. Thorn's cruiser pulled into the driveway seconds later. He jumped out of the car and rushed toward us.

"Can you give us an escort to the hospital?" Kurt asked Thorn.

"What happened?" Thorn asked.

"She cut her hand. I'm taking her to the emergency room. Can you give us an escort?"

"Let me have a look at it," Thorn said. "Let's take her back inside and wash it off before we go running off to the hospital."

I understood why Thorn said it. He knew Remy and Annika could heal me, but he didn't think about the fact that we'd probably already been over that argument.

"What is up with you people?" Kurt asked in frustration.

He was genuinely concerned for my safety, and didn't realize that my friends could help me. I appreciated it even if he was misguided.

"Let her go., Thorn sort of growled.

That snapped me back into focus. I looked up at Thorn and was taken aback. It looked like he hadn't slept. There were dark circles under his eyes, his hair was a mess, and his uniform looked dirty and rumpled. He looked like he needed to be at home taking a nap and not out working.

"I don't know what's going on around here, but right now, I'm worried about Brighton losing the use of her hand. So I'm taking her to the hospital. How anyone could have a problem with that is beyond me."

By then, Bobby, Rachel, and Link had all come outside. The took a few steps toward us, and Link actually put himself in between Thorn and Kurt.

"It's okay, Thorn," Remy said. "I was going to ride with her. We'll get her to the hospital and get her fixed up right away."

"You butt out of this," Thorn snarled.

"Thorn. It's okay," I said firmly.

"Yeah, man. It's cool," Link said. "Let's just take this down a notch."

"I decide when to take things down a notch," Thorn said.

He grabbed Kurt's arm and tried to yank him away from me. Kurt shook him off, but when he did, Thorn stumbled back into Link.

I wouldn't know until later when I watched the footage Toto had begun to record what happened because it was all confusing. But the end result was a scuffle where Thorn ended up throwing a punch at Kurt. Kurt shoved him back.

"That's it, you're under arrest," Thorn shouted.

"Thorn, no," Remy said in a commanding voice that I wasn't sure I'd ever get used to hearing. "You're out of line, and you're on video. I'd suggest you leave and let Kurt and I get Brighton to the hospital."

Either because he was completely in shock or because Remy was using some magic to subdue his temper, Thorn backed off. He looked completely stunned, but my hand hurt. I didn't want to stick around.

Once we were on the way to the hospital, and Kurt's eyes and attention were on the road, Remy used some healing magic to stop the pain and heal the worst of the damage. I stopped him before he could heal it completely because it would have been too hard to explain, but with the pain gone, the injury was far easier for me to deal with.

After a couple of hours of waiting and a few stiches, I was released from the ER to go home. Annika and Brody stayed at Hangman's House and helped Meri keep an eye on the Ghost Seekers who'd stayed behind.

They were all sitting around the living room when we got back. Rachel looked at me through slightly narrowed eyes when we walked into the house.

"Did you go to the emergency room or the salon?" she asked.

"What?" I asked.

"Your hair is different. It was bright red when you left, and now it's got pink streaks in it."

I self-consciously pushed a strand that had fallen out of my bun back over my ear. My hair was changing color again, and Rachel noticed.

"I had pink streaks in it before. They just show up in different light, and when I tie it back. My ponytails are usually neat to cover it, but this bun is messy."

"Oh, yeah. I've seen photos of that stuff on social media. Where people have hair color hidden. Cool," she said. I got the weird feeling that she didn't entirely believe me, but at least that I'd dodged the bullet for the time being.

"So what's on the agenda for tonight?" I asked. "Another overnight in the cemetery? You guys still haven't investigated the old cemetery officially either."

"We were thinking of something else," Bobby said.

"Well, it's probably too late to start something in the courthouse. What about the abandoned asylum?" I asked.

"That's not in Coventry," Chris interjected.

"I know," I said. "It's in the next town, but it's close. I'm sure your viewers would love it."

"We were actually hoping you'd let us do an investigation here," Kurt said softly.

"No," Remy said before I could answer. "I knew letting you guys in here was a mistake."

"We aren't trying to upset you," Toto said. "I'll even let you review any footage before we put it in the show."

"You have to understand that this is one of the most fascinating locations in Coventry," Chris said. "The history of this place is amazing."

"Don't," Annika warned.

"Don't what?" I asked.

"She doesn't know," Chris's voice didn't hide his shock. "She doesn't know about the house."

"I mean, I know it's called Hangman's House," I said. "I guess I never really thought too much about why."

"That's weird," Brody said as he came down the stairs. "I didn't really think about looking into the house's history either."

I wondered if the witches of Coventry had used magic to keep me from looking into the history of the house, or perhaps Meri did. The again, with the way the house behaved, it could have been responsible for Brody's and my complete lack of interest.

"You should know," Kurt said. "You live here, after all."

What they told me next was shocking, but it wasn't surprising. Before Coventry was a town full of witches, it was a frontier village. Hangman's House belonged to the first wealthy family in the area. The head of the household eventually became the mayor and the town judge because back then, people were pretty much left to run things the way they wanted out on the prairie. As long as what they did didn't draw the attention of the magistrates in the larger cities, small hamlets like pre-colonial Coventry did things the way the wanted.

And at one point, what they wanted was witch trials. That year there had been a great deal of sickness and a lot of the crops had gone bad too.

One evening, the youngest son of the mayor had snuck out of his bedroom to go for a walk on their property. Some said he'd endured a belting that evening for having a smart mouth and was probably in a sour mood. He was looking to take his hurt and humiliation out on someone.

He found several someones as he skirted the edge of his father's property near the woods. The boy heard laughter and saw a fire in the woods, and he was drawn to see what it was.

What he came upon was a small group of the town's young, unmarried women dancing around a small fire in a clearing. They were drinking wine and singing.

Of course, the boy ran back to his father and reported that he'd seen the girls worshiping the devil in the woods. The mayor was more than willing to forgive his son for sneaking out given the information he'd found for his father.

The next day, a meeting was called at the church, and shortly after, the girls were all arrested. Their families were afraid to protest, and most of them ended up testifying against the girls.

The trials lasted less than a week, and the entire group was sentenced to hang. No one stepped in to prevent the executions, so all of the girls were hung the next Sunday afternoon right after church.

"And they call this Hangman's House because the judge who sentenced them to hang lived here," I said.

"Yes, and from what I've put together, the girls are buried across the street in the unmarked cemetery," Chris said. "It's mostly Tuttlesmith and Skeenbauer ancestors in the old part, but there are a few graves there that are much older."

"Where did they hang?" I didn't want to know, but the question was burning a hole in my mind.

"The tree out front," Rachel said matter-of-factly.

The rest of the Ghost Seekers' heads swiveled around. Kurt glared at her. I got the feeling they hadn't wanted to tell me that part.

"Oh," I said and turned to Remy and Annika. "Why didn't you tell me this?"

"It wasn't important," Annika said. "I mean, of course it was an important part of history, but it's not like they were real witches."

"What do you mean by that?" Bobby asked.

"I mean that there have been numerous witch hunts and trials throughout history where innocent women died because people were scared of things they didn't understand," Annika said.

"And you?" I asked Brody. "This never came up?"

"It's not his fault," Remy said. "Most of that information is contained in the Coventry archives and a few rare books. It's not exactly common knowledge."

"But you guys know?" I asked the Ghost Seekers.

"We don't have access to a small town's private archives," Kurt said, "but we do have access to something else. We're able to get information most other people can't or don't want."

"What do you mean?"

"What he means is that we get our information from the dark web," Rachel said. "There are forums there where people can post and discuss real paranormal evidence. No one there accuses them of hoaxes or being crazy. We just investigate."

"Sometimes we have to pay for information too," Link added. "Some people have information or evidence you can only see if you pay."

"That doesn't sound like it would be very reliable," Brody said.

"It's not usually, but sometimes you get something good," Kurt said. "Like the information on this house. We weren't sure if it was true, but your friend confirmed it. That means there was another set of witch trials in this country."

"There were probably even more than that," Chris added. "The ones in Salem were only discovered because they affected people beyond just the village of Salem."

"But if I let you investigate the house, then the information about the witch trials will get out," I said. "The world will know."

"Don't you think it should?" Kurt asked.

I knew it was a decision I'd be making for the whole town. On one hand, I knew it would draw more investigators and possibly tourists to Coventry. On the other hand, Kurt was right. I felt like the world should know.

"All right, you can do an investigation on the property," I said. "But if I catch anyone rifling through my underwear drawer, it's over."

Kurt clapped his hands together. "Yes! Thank you so much, Brighton. After we conduct our investigation here tonight, we can move on to the old cemetery tomorrow. This is going to be awesome."

Later while they were setting up, Remy pulled me aside. "I thought you were supposed to be making things boring and getting them to leave."

"Well, I'm not very good at stuff like that," I said. "I assume that you and Annika will hang around and help me keep them in line?"

"Oh, I wouldn't miss this for the world," Annika said from behind me.

The first place they wanted to investigate was the basement. Of course, I had a load of laundry going in the dryer and the Ghost Seekers just had to wait. Paranormal investigation or not, I wasn't going to let my clothes mold in the dryer. I hated when I forgot them and had to rewash everything with vinegar.

While the dryer finished, Link and Bobby set up the lighting for the basement. Meri was down there watching everything going on, and I was glad. The Ghost Seekers didn't know that there was the possibility that a demon might appear down there, but Meri would protect us.

It wasn't something I had to worry about myself because any demons that wanted to come into the house that way needed a way in, but I had to wonder if having all of those people down there would be their way in. All of that energy and the Ghost Seekers calling out to entities. Had I made a mistake?

"What are you doing?" I asked when I noticed that Bobby was doing something in the middle of the basement floor.

He was setting up candles. Then he pulled out a piece of white chalk and started to draw a circle.

"It's just for show," Bobby said with a shrug as he drew a pentagram in the middle of the circle. "It's not like we're really going to try and summon any demons."

That annoyed me a little because while it was possible to summon demons by forming a circle, goddess knew I'd done that recently, it was the only reason for casting one. I debated telling him that he was messing around with things he didn't understand.

But that didn't make sense either. Of course, they understood what they were doing. The Ghost Seekers were paranormal researchers. They probably knew more about the occult than I did. Bobby had to know that he was mocking witchcraft in a house where a man had murdered women for being witches. He was trying to antagonize the ghosts, or he really was trying to give something more sinister power.

"Hey," Kurt said as he descended the basement stairs. "Seriously, Bobby? We talked about this before. We agreed as a group that we weren't going to do any of this stuff anymore. It makes the show look like we're going for cheap thrills, and you know that it's disrespectful."

"No, we didn't agree. You agreed and everybody thought they had to go along with it," Bobby said resentfully.

"You should have said something about it when we had the meeting, Bobby," Kurt said. "This issue has already been decided."

"I kinda agree with Bobby," Rachel said.

I watched as Link and Toto sort of took a step back. They obviously didn't want to be involved. Chris spoke up next.

"I'm not sure why you guys want to do this," he said. "We know that messing around with the occult can have bad results. We said when we started this show we weren't going to use cheap scare tactics or creative editing to fuel ratings. Then when things were slow, we fudged on that promise a little. And where did it get us?"

"It got us attacked," Kurt responded.

"We weren't attacked," Bobby argued. "It's not like a demon came out of the woodwork and started strangling us or something like that. You're being dramatic."

"What happened to us could have just been bad luck," Rachel said. "It could have all been a coincidence."

"We all know that none of that was a coincidence," Kurt's voice was just above a whisper.

"Hey, man, I'm with Kurt," Link finally spoke up. "You know it was something more. It was bad. Think about Toto. He'd never had that sleep paralysis crap in his life, and how long did he have to suffer with that? Huh? Do you guys really want to put us in that position again? And what about you, Rachel? What about what you went through?"

"That wasn't because of some entity," she said.

"You know it was." Kurt sounded upset. "You admitted it back then. You're just rationalizing now."

While they were arguing, I noticed that Meri had moved to the edge of the circle. He sat there with his tail swishing over the chalk circle Bobby had drawn. I could tell he wanted to say something, but he couldn't.

"I'm going to run to the restroom while you guys figure this out," I said and started up the basement steps.

Meri darted up after me and followed me until we were in the bathroom. I closed and locked the door behind us.

"I can't stay up where long," he said. "There's something trying to come through down there. It's feeding off their fighting."

"Well, you have to get rid of it. I know you can," I said.

"I can't with them there. There's a reason I never do it in front of you. It's not because it's some secret I don't want you to know. It could harm you. It could harm them.
You've got to get them to move out of the basement, and if they are going to do their little investigation down there, they have to do it without the circle and candles.
They're playing with fire."

"I'll figure something out."

Chapter Four

When I went back downstairs, things had gotten so tense that the Ghost Seekers weren't talking anymore. Instead, they were standing there glaring at each other. You could have cut the tension around them with a knife.

"Hey, guys, why don't we go outside and get some air," I said. "We could go do an investigation around the tree. I'll help."

I didn't really want to help them investigate the hanging tree, but if it got them out of the basement, it was worth it. I just hoped I didn't anger the spirits of the women who died there too much as I still had to live in the house after the Ghost Seekers finally left.

"Nah. I'm outta here," Bobby said before brushing past me and pounding up the stairs.

"I'll go after him," Rachel said after a few seconds of everyone standing around in stunned silence.

"I'm getting a little tired of you siding with him over me," Kurt called after her.

"I'm doing it for the show," she snapped back.

"You guys go upstairs," Kurt said. "I'm going to clean up his mess."

"I'll help you," I said, not wanting to leave him alone in the basement with a demon trying to come through the veil.

"Me too," Remy said. "Let's get it done."

It only took a couple of minutes to sweep away the chalk drawing, but even in that short amount of time, the air had begun to go cold. The smell of sulfur tickled my nose, and the hair on the back of my neck stood up.

Kurt got kind of a strange look on his face. I thought he was going to want to investigate what was happening.

"Let's get upstairs and see how things are going," he said.

It surprised me, but I wasn't going to question it. The last thing I needed was the remaining Ghost Seekers filing down to my basement to catch a demon crossing the veil on film.

Kurt, Remy, and I all went upstairs while Meri stayed behind. I left the door open a crack for my familiar to escape once he'd worked his magic. I knew what he did could be loud, so I put up a spell to make any non-witches in the house ignore any sound that came from the basement. It was kind of like a ward against noise, and I hoped it worked.

Chris, Toto, and Link were in the living room with Annika and Brody. We all sat around a fire that Remy built. Meri was there shortly after. He curled up on the back of the sofa and took a snooze, so I guessed that his mission had been a success.

"Should we be worried that they haven't come back yet?" I asked when Rachel and Bobby didn't return for over an hour.

"I wouldn't worry about them," Toto said. "He gets himself all tied up in knots sometimes. They'll be back."

"I can't believe he's doing this now," Kurt said. "We have one of the best opportunities in our careers, and he's off throwing a fit."

"I hate to bring it up," Chris said, "but how many more times are we going to let him do this?"

"We've discussed this. I'm not ready to fire him," Kurt said.

"You mean Rachel doesn't want you to fire him," Chris said. "I don't know why that doesn't bother you."

"They're friends," Kurt said. "They were friends before she and I got together, and yeah, part of it is Rachel. I don't want to upset her, and I don't want to lose her from the show either."

"She won't quit," Toto said. "Rachel won't be happy, but she's not going to quit. She needs this job."

"We all need this job," Link said.

"Yeah, and if we get canceled because of Bobby's temper, it's going to hurt us all,"

Chris said. "You admitted yourself the last time we discussed this that the show would be better without him. He was great at first, but now we have to edit out so much of his unprofessional crap."

"Let's finish this season," Kurt said. "His contract is up for renewal after this one, and that would make things far less messy."

"Seems fair," Toto said.

"Yeah," both Chris and Link agreed.

We sat around waiting for them to come back for a couple more hours. Kurt called Rachel at one point, and she said she had it under control. He seemed annoyed after that.

"I think we should leave and go get a room at the inn," Kurt said to me. "We're not going to be able to do an investigation tonight. There's no point in keeping you up for this. Thank you for everything."

"You can stay," I said and then bit my tongue. A little too late. "I have enough room."

"What?" Remy asked before any of the Ghost Seekers had a chance.

"You'll get everything worked out and get the investigation done tomorrow," I said. "I'm sure it will be fine."

"I'm staying too," Annika said. "Slumber party."

"You don't have to do that," Kurt said.

"I know I don't have to, but I'm offering," I said.

"I guess it would be good to wait here for Bobby and Rachel," Kurt said.

"Great. The spare rooms are upstairs. Let me show you."

After I showed them their rooms, everybody went back downstairs to the living room to wait. We sat around talking for a while, but at some point, I must have drifted off.

When I woke up, dawn was breaking and it was just me and Meri on the sofa. I figured Annika was asleep in my room. At least I hoped that's where she was and not in Brody's room.

Remy wasn't there, and I wondered if he'd gone home. I checked the kitchen for him first, but there wasn't anyone there.

I thought about texting him, but I decided to check the driveway first. If his car was gone, that meant he'd gone home. I'd text him and ask him if he wanted to come back for breakfast before the investigation began.

There was a text from Thorn on my phone, and I realized he hadn't come by the night before or called. *Got caught up with some stuff. Love ya* – that was the entire message.

Love you too – was what I messaged back.

There was nothing from Remy, but I could only assume he hadn't wanted to wake me up. I went to the front door and opened it to look outside.

His car wasn't in the driveway, but it was such a nice morning, I had to step out onto the porch to get some fresh air and early morning sunshine.

I stretched my arms above my head and closed my eyes as I tilted my head and face toward the sun. I noticed the Ghost Seekers' van was parked in front of my house again, so I knew Bobby and Rachel must have returned at some point that night.

It was when I surveyed the rest of the yard that I got a shock. What I saw I would never forget. At first, I thought someone had TPed the tree in the front yard.

My breath caught in my throat when I realized it was a person hanging from the tree. "Stop it," I said because I thought it was a spirit trying to scare me. "That's not funny."

But then something else occurred to me. I recognized the clothes the person was wearing. "Annika!" I called out because she was the first person I could think of who would help me. "Annika, I need help!"

I dialed the phone to call Thorn and ran across the lawn. The man was up in the tree and I couldn't reach him. "Thorn, you have to come to my house right now. He's dead."

Just as I was about to tell Thorn who it was, the wind blew and the body swayed in the tree above me as the branch groaned loudly. It snapped, and I dropped the phone as I dove out of the way.

"Brighton, are you okay?" Annika yelled as she ran out the front door.

"I'm okay. I just... I couldn't get him down, but the tree branch broke," I mumbled.

I was on the ground, and my legs felt like jelly. Annika sank down beside me and wrapped her arm around my shoulder. "Did you call Thorn?" she asked and pushed back a strand of hair that was plastered with sweat across my forehead.

"I did."

"Kurt!" The first of the Ghost Seekers came rushing out the front door.

It was Chris. He was still dressed in pajama pants with a blue diamond pattern and a white t-shirt, but he raced across the lawn and knelt down next to his friend.

"He's dead," Chris said. "He was in the tree?"

"He was," I said. "The wind blew, and he just fell. He almost fell on me."

My head felt fuzzy, and my fingers were tingling. I'd later figure out that I was going into shock. Not because of finding Kurt, but the combination of finding him like that and having his body almost fall on me was too much. Probably because I was already under so much stress because of the Thorn thing.

"What are you doing?" I asked when Annika grabbed my phone.

"Calling Remy," she said. "He should be here."

"We should all get away," I said. "It's a crime scene."

Annika helped me to my feet, and we all retreated to the porch to wait for Thorn. When he arrived, Thorn got out of his cruiser and walked over to where Kurt lay on the ground.

"I'm going to make coffee," I said, suddenly feeling antsy.

I wasn't sure what it was, but something about the way Thorn ignored me when he showed up made me feel nervous. I knew he had a job to do, but he didn't even look at me.

"I think I'll make some food," I said to Remy.

He'd come into the house and walked into the kitchen while I was pouring myself a cup of coffee. A look of concern darkened his face.

"Okay, I'll help," he said. "But maybe not a full spread like yesterday. You're doing so much for these people, and you're supposed to be running them off."

"We'll just do some bacon and toast then?"

"Sounds like a plan. Why don't you do the toast and I'll handle the bacon," Remy said.

"Thank you."

"Oh, I don't mind. I like bacon. I'll probably steal a couple of extra pieces since I'm cooking it," he said with a soft smile.

"No, I mean not for the bacon. I mean, I am grateful you're helping me with breakfast," I sort of stammered. "I mean thank you for being here. Thank you for coming right away when Annika called and for being here for me."

He'd been getting a pan out of the cabinet, but Remy set it down. He walked over and pulled me into a hug. "Always," he whispered so softly I almost thought I'd imagined it.

"Did I hear my name when I came through the front door?" Annika asked as she barreled into the kitchen. "Oh. Sorry guys. Hey wait, group hug!" she exclaimed and wrapped her arms around us.

Annika went outside to tell the Ghost Seekers that there was food and coffee. Brody came down after smelling the coffee but was completely unaware of what had happened. We filled him in while we ate.

Eventually, there was a knock at the front door. I went to see who it was and was surprised to find Thorn standing on the other side.

"You could have just come in," I said.

"I'm here as the sheriff," he said. "I didn't think it was appropriate to just walk in."

"Okay. So what's going on?"

I didn't want to look over where the body was, but I couldn't help it. The coroner already had Kurt covered and was taking him away. That was a bit of a relief.

"The coroner has ruled it a suicide," Thorn said.

"What? No. No way. He wasn't suicidal," I said.

"There's no evidence of anything else, Brighton," he said and pinched the bridge of his nose. "I've got to go back to the station and fill out a mountain of paperwork. Um. I'll call you later, okay?"

"Okay," I said.

And then he turned and left. It almost took my breath away to just watch him walk off like that, but I managed to hold it together. I wiped away one tear that managed to escape just as Toto stood up from his spot on the front steps.

"I should get the rest of our stuff out of your house," he said.

"Are you leaving town?" I asked.

"I don't know what we're going to do yet," he said. "We're going to go get a room at the inn and get out of your hair while we decide."

"You don't have to do that," I said. "I'm supposed to be your guide while you're in town. I'd rather if we just stayed here, if you don't mind. Unless you guys want some alone time, but you don't really need to pay for a room for that."

"We don't want to put you out anymore than we already have," Chris said as he joined him.

"Well, there's food and coffee inside. Please come in and eat. I would never put you out after something like this," I said.

It was so quiet that you could almost hear people chewing their bacon in the house. No one said a word, and the air felt heavy and sad.

Then Rachel broke the spell. "I think it was a ghost," she said. "I think something from this house attacked him."

"Wait just a second," Remy cautioned. "There's nothing supernatural that could have done that to him."

"What if he was possessed?" she said. "What if one of the ghosts possessed him and got him to kill himself?"

"If it did, it's because of that crap in the basement," Toto said. "Kurt warned you, and he paid the price for your mistakes."

"Hey, don't talk to her like that," Bobby snapped.

"Guys," I said. "Please don't fight."

"Don't worry about us," Rachel snarled. "We're going over to the cemetery across the street to do some investigative work. We'll get to the bottom of this. I intend to find every shred of evidence that a ghost from this house killed Kurt. And we don't need a babysitter."

"Kurt just died," Link said. "Don't you think we should put the show on hold for a bit. At least until after the funeral?"

"No," Rachel said. "Absolutely not. Kurt would want the show to go on."

"I'm going with her," Bobby said. "Anybody that wants to join us, and be a part of a historical paranormal investigation, you know where to find us."

"What a jerk," Toto said as soon as Bobby and Rachel were out the door.

"I can't believe they're doing this," Chris said softly. "Did he really just indicate that they are going to use Kurt's death for ratings? Is that what I heard?"

"Maybe they're just in shock and possibly denial," Link offered, but his words where half-hearted.

"What are we going to do?" Chris asked.

"What if she was right?" I said cautiously. "What if Kurt didn't actually kill himself?"

I knew it was a crazy thing to suggest, but I believed it. It wasn't that I believed that a ghost had possessed Kurt and made him hang himself, though that was still certainly possible, but it was more that I got the feeling someone had murdered him.

Who that was, I felt compelled to figure out. He'd died at my home. Not only would the news raise the eyebrows of the residents of Coventry, but the world at large too. If Rachel's narrative that Kurt killed himself at Hangman's House because of a possession got wings, paranormal investigators would flock to my town. If that dam broke, nothing could stop it.

One thing that could stop it was proof that he hadn't killed himself. I could provide that if I could prove he was murdered.

Chapter Five

"Can I talk to you?" I asked as soon as Thorn picked up the phone. "Can we meet?"

"I'm supposed to spend time with Dani after work," he said. "I'm sorry, and I promise that we'll get together when things settle down."

"Settle down?" I asked skeptically. "You think that having a child is going to settle down anytime before your daughter is an adult?"

"Brighton, please," he said with a sigh. "I was really hoping you would be supportive of all of this."

"I'm trying," I said. "But you're not giving me any opportunity to be supportive. Look, what about lunch? Surely you weren't planning on having lunch with your daughter, right? Can you meet me for lunch?"

I kinda hated myself for begging him to spend time with me, but I wanted to talk to Thorn about the murder. He'd probably be unhappy when he found out why I wanted to get together, but whatever. He wasn't exactly focused on my happiness either.

I knew that was probably unfair, but it was how I felt. It wasn't my fault any of it was happening, and while I knew it wasn't Thorn's fault either, I also knew there was no way that I'd have just dropped him the way he had me. I knew in my heart that I would have tried to be so much more considerate of his feelings, and it hurt me that he wasn't doing the same for me.

"Okay," he said curtly. "Where do you want to meet?"

"Are you near the park?" I asked. "We could meet there. I'll bring lunch."

"That would be all right." Thorn's voice had softened some. "I'll meet you in an hour?"

"Yes, I'll see you then. Love you."

"You too," he said and hung up.

I set the phone down on the counter and took a deep breath. Something wasn't right with Thorn, but I had to wonder if I was putting too much of myself into a relationship that hadn't been going on for that long. Sure, there were strong feelings involved, but I had to wonder what I was doing to myself. Part of me knew he hadn't earned my patience with all the grief he was putting me through, but that part of me wasn't very loud yet.

"I wasn't eavesdropping," Remy said.

I looked up and he was standing in the doorway to the kitchen. I'd been feeling completely unsteady after hanging up the phone, but Remy's presence instantly comforted me.

"I know you weren't," I said.

"Do you want to talk about it?"

"I think I'm just meeting with him to discuss the case," I said. "It's important for Coventry that we convince the authorities that it wasn't a suicide. If we can't, and Rachel and Bobby run with this ghost possession suicide theory, it's going to be a mess."

"You don't have to pretend like you don't want to see him on my account," Remy said and took a step into the kitchen.

"I don't think I'm pretending," I said. "He retreats when things get hard, and I don't know that I can deal with that. I thought I could. I mean, he promised he wouldn't do it anymore. You saw all of this coming, and I didn't listen."

"This isn't what I saw," Remy said. "Not like this."

"Then what did you see?" I asked. "Never mind. I don't want to know. If I know, then it could just become some self-fulfilling prophecy. Let's make some sandwiches."

"Only if I get one too," Remy said with a reassuring smile.

"We'll see," I said.

He pulled me close and gave me a hug. It felt good to have someone want to hug me as much as Remy did. After that, we made sandwiches and little bags of chips. We didn't talk while we worked. Remy and I didn't always have to talk. I never wanted to forget how nice it was just to be there working alongside him.

I got to the park before Thorn and found a bench that was in a quiet spot. The bench was toward the back of the park near a line of trees that marked the beginning of a wooded area, but I could still see the parking area.

Thorn arrived a few minutes after me, and I watched as he pulled his cruiser into a parking spot. He got out and looked around for me, and I waved to him once he looked in my direction.

He smiled at me and waved back. It was almost as unexpected as the heart flutter I got from it.

Thorn made his way over to me quickly and took his place beside me on the bench. "Sorry I was so short earlier. I haven't been sleeping well, but I need to remember not to take that out on you."

"I understand," I said. "I brought food."

"Oh, good. I'm starving."

"You're not eating well."

"I've been spending most of my off time with Dani, but I haven't wanted to eat with her and Sadie. I don't want to give Dani the impression that we're all going to be together, so I guess I just haven't been eating," he said.

"It must be difficult," I offered.

"It has been," Thorn said. "I honestly don't know how I feel about all of this yet. I haven't had time to process my thoughts on it, but that shouldn't be your concern."

"How can it not be my concern, Thorn?"

"I mean, we'll have to figure it out eventually, but I have to figure it out first," he said with a sigh. "We don't have to talk about this if you don't want to."

I took that as meaning he didn't want to talk about it, so I dropped it. The truth was, I didn't want to talk about it either.

"I do want to talk to you about Kurt's death," I said softly.

"Brighton, really?" Thorn was obviously annoyed.

"What?" I asked a little more curtly than I intended. "I was supposed to be their chaperone, and one of them turned up dead on my watch. Rachel is saying she thinks a spirit possessed him and made him commit suicide. If they run with that idea for their show, I can't even imagine all of the repercussions for Coventry."

"So you want to pretend like he was murdered just to keep that from happening?"

"I wouldn't be pretending, Thorn. I really do think he was murdered. Kurt wasn't suicidal."

"Maybe it really was one of the spirits in your house," he said more to himself than to me.

"No. It wasn't that."

"How do you know?" he asked.

"I just do. It's my house, Thorn. If something like that was there, Meri and I would know." But did I know that?

He'd made me doubt my conviction, and I couldn't let that happen. My intuition told me that someone, a live person, had killed Kurt. I'd get to the bottom of it with or without Thorn.

"I'm sorry I upset you," he said. "Thank you for bringing me lunch."

After that we sat and ate our sandwiches in silence. With every moment that went by, I felt the distance between us turning into a gorge until Thorn finally tried to bridge it.

"I haven't been good to you," he said.

"It's only been a couple of days," I said.

And there it was. I was doing it again. I'd done the same thing with my ex-husband, Donnie. He'd neglect me or make me feel small, and I'd try to make him feel better.

"You wouldn't leave me hanging the way I've left you," he said and took my hand.

"Not even for a couple of days. Not in a situation as intense as this one. I know that I've said I'd do better, and I really will. Would you be terribly upset if I came by tonight for dinner after my shift?"

"Not at all," I said. "But be aware that I've got a house full."

"Well, maybe we should wait then," Thorn said.

"No reason for that. I don't mind if you don't."

"All right then. It's a date."

Before I could say anything else, Thorn's radio squawked to life. He had a call he had to take. As he was leaving, he asked me a question that made the whole uncomfortable lunch scene worth it.

"When you found Kurt this morning, were there any gloves on the ground or in the tree?"

"No," I said.

"You didn't pick up a pair or perhaps see someone else pick them up?"

"Nope. Why?"

"Oh, it's just that the coroner made a comment that he'd expected to see scrapes on Kurt's hands given how high he'd climbed. He didn't know how he'd gotten himself up there without any scrapes on his palms and without gloves, but I assume he was just careful. Or perhaps he had callused hands," Thorn said before kissing me quickly and heading off.

But the callused hands thing didn't seem reasonable to me. If that were the case, then the coroner wouldn't have made the comment about the lack of scrapes. It was possible that he'd just been careful or lucky climbing the old tree, but it was also possible that he was murdered.

I went home with Rachel on my mind. She'd been very quick to offer the theory that Kurt had been possessed and committed suicide. Maybe just a little too quick.

Chapter Six

"Okay, the first thing I want to do is go ahead with the investigation of this house," Rachel said nearly as soon as I'd walked through the front door. "We need to find the spirit that killed Kurt while the site is still hot."

"Rachel, come on," Chris said. "Kurt died this morning."

"And what is sitting around going to do? Waiting isn't going to make him any less dead."

"I think you're in shock. You don't want to make decisions you'll regret," Toto said.

"I won't regret doing my job," Rachel said. "It's what Kurt would want. He would want the show to go on and be a success. He wouldn't want us moping around and ruining our careers because he died."

"Well, maybe we're not up to it," Chris said. "Maybe some of us need some time."

"Some time for what?" Rachel's question sounded like an accusation. "I think there is a spirit in this house that killed him, and I'd think you'd want to get to the bottom of it."

"I really don't think there is a spirit in this house that killed Kurt," I said.

"Well, we'll find that out one way or another," Rachel retorted. "You did say that we could do the investigation here. Are you backing out?"

"I'm not. I just don't think that looking for a murderous spirit is the best way to run things," I said.

"This is my show. I appreciate your concern, but I can handle this," she said.

"Whoa, wait just a second, Rachel. What do you mean this is your show?" Chris asked.

"Yeah, what are you talking about Rachel? This is our show," Toto said. "Kurt dying doesn't make it your show."

"Well, he was the showrunner, and he and I were going to be married. So I think that means that it passes to me," she said.

"He wasn't a king," Chris said. "Showrunner doesn't pass to his heirs. It's in our contracts what happens if one of us dies, and when Kurt died, his creative responsibilities pass to me."

"No way," Rachel said.

"Yes way," Toto said in support of Chris.

"Yeah, Rachel. I know you and Kurt were close, but it's my job to decide how the show proceeds from here," Chris said.

"This is why I never wanted to sell out to a stupid studio," Bobby said. "This is ridiculous."

"Without selling out to the studio, *Ghost Seekers* would still be a YouTube-only show that we all had to do part-time after our crappy jobs," Chris reminded them. "Besides, we all took a vote before we signed our contracts."

"Yeah, but we didn't know what was in your contract," Rachel said to Chris. "Why weren't the rest of us included?"

"Because the studio made these decisions as part of taking on the show, and we never really thought it would happen. Nobody thought Kurt would die," Chris said.

"So what's it going to be, boss man? What do we do next?" Rachel's contempt was palpable.

"I want to talk to our hostess alone for a few minutes," Chris said.

He cocked his eyebrow up while looking at me, and I knew he as asking my permission. "Sure," I said. "In the kitchen?"

Both Rachel and Bobby let out exasperated huffs. Link and Toto headed for the front door.

"We're going to head over to that coffee place and grab the strongest sludge they can make for us," Link said. "We'll be back in a few minutes."

"Bobby and I are going to go over to the old cemetery across the road, but don't worry, we won't do any real investigating without mom around," Rachel said sarcastically.

"What are you going to do with us?" Annika asked.

I motioned for her and Remy to follow me into the kitchen. If Chris wanted to talk to me, he could talk to all three of us.

"I'll make more coffee," I said as the other three sat down at the kitchen table.

"I wanted to talk to you guys alone because I think we're going to have a problem with Rachel," Chris said. "I don't know any less blunt way of putting it. She's not handling Kurt's death well. Which is to be expected. I just thought she'd take some time to grieve instead of wanting to dive back into the show."

"Maybe if you talk to her," I offered.

"No. The only person who could rein her in was Kurt. There is zero chance she'll listen to me, Link, or Toto. Bobby won't be any help because he'll do whatever she wants. I know it's completely inappropriate for me to ask you to let us do the investigation, but I don't know any other way."

"What do you mean?" Remy asked before I had the chance.

"I mean that if you don't let her, she'll go live on YouTube with her theory. She'll tell the world that a ghost possessed Kurt and forced him to commit suicide. Rachel has her own following," Chris continued. "They're… darker than the usual *Ghost Seekers* fans. She'll rile up her followers, and tomorrow Coventry will be swimming with them."

"And you think that if we do the investigation and it turns up nothing, she'll back off?" I asked.

"I think it's the only chance you've got right now."

"I don't understand this," I said. "Why wouldn't she want to wait until at least after the funeral? Is it just shock? I can't understand pushing through. He just died."

"Because she doesn't care," Annika observed casually. "Sorry to be so blunt, but I get the feeling she doesn't give a crap he died. You keep saying it's shock, but that's not the vibe that chick is putting off."

"There relationship did seem a little rough around the edges, but I don't know if I want to go as far as to say she doesn't care that he died," Chris said.

"It's okay," I said. "Either way, it's fine with me if you go forward with the investigation, as long as you guys are up for it. I can tell her no if you need me to."

"No, it's fine," Chris said. "We'll do this now. It hasn't really hit me yet that he's gone, but I know it will. I guess it would be better to get the season wrapped up before it does. I'll need to call Kurt's parents, but I believe it would be better for everyone if we got the finale finished before we need to go home for his funeral. That will give us a couple of days."

When Toto and Link got back from their coffee run, Chris briefed them on our decision. They reluctantly agreed to participate. I could tell that Toto was taking it much harder than Link, and I wondered if Grateful Dead was in shock like Chris. Toto had red rings around his eyes. He'd been crying while they were gone.

"I'll go over and get them," Chris said.

"Toto and I will get the equipment from the basement and set up around the rest of the house," Link said.

Rachel looked around after everything was set up. I could tell by her pinched expression that she wasn't pleased.

"Let's wait until tonight," she said. "There's no atmosphere with all this light."

Chris groaned. "Seriously?"

"We can do the courthouse during the day. That was supposed to be on our schedule, and we have to do it during the day. So let's do it now. Is that still okay?" she'd directed the question at me and Remy.

"Sure," Remy said.

"Hey, do you guys have this for now?" Annika asked. "I need to go open my shop."

"Yeah, we've got it," I said.

"Cool, I'll be back after I close. Wouldn't miss tonight for the world."

After that, the remaining Ghost Seekers loaded up in their van, and Remy drove us to the courthouse. "Do you have to go to work?" I asked as we pulled into our parking space.

"I think the archives can survive without me for a day," he said. "I would hope the council would appreciate that I am helping you protect the town."

Once we were all gathered around the courthouse lobby, I addressed the Ghost Seekers. The town council had decided they could do a ghost hunt at the courthouse, but there were rules.

"Okay, guys. So courthouse investigation is a courtesy. There are rules we have to follow. If we don't, then the council has no problem getting security to throw us out. The first rule is that the archives are Remy's, so you can go down there, but it's his show. The top floor is the council's offices. We can go up there as long as we aren't too loud, but we have to stay out of the council members' offices. So that's pretty much the hallway and the conference rooms that aren't in use. The middle floors are courtrooms and more conference rooms. We can go in any of those that aren't in use. And finally, you have to stay with me at all times while you're investigating here. So we all have to stay together."

"Sounds like a blast," Rachel said and rolled her eyes.

I wanted to say something to her about how her attitude wasn't helping her friends, but I hoped she was just struggling with her boyfriend's death. I didn't want to be a jerk to someone who had just suffered such a huge loss, so I let it go.

What I didn't let go was the suspicion that had begun to niggle at my brain. Rachel had taken off to find Bobby the night before, I didn't know where she'd been with Kurt died. I assumed she'd have come back to my house and slept, but I didn't know that for sure. It also struck me as strange that, if she had come to my home and slept, how did she not know that Kurt left the house that morning? Perhaps it was because they didn't sleep in the same room. I could understand that, but I needed to know for sure.

"Why don't we start in the basement?" Chris suggested. "I'd like to send Toto and Link downstairs with the camera and the boom mike and get shots of me coming off the elevator."

"What about us?" Bobby asked.

"Well, while I'm talking about some of the history of the courthouse, you and Rachel can record audio. We'll take several opportunities to cut to Rachel doing EVP. Bobby, we'll have you with the EMF reader. You can look for electrical anomalies and jump in if anyone sees, hears, or feels anything unusual."

On the elevator down, Remy turned to me with a serious look on his face. "I've got to tell you something. There's... uh... something about the archives I never told you."

I looked over quickly at Link and Toto. They just gave me a shrug, but it looked like they already knew. So it wasn't something Remy couldn't share with them, but it was something I didn't know. Awesome.

"What is it?" I asked cautiously, but I was sure I didn't really want to know.

"So, uh, back when the courthouse was built, the basement wasn't used as an archive," he said.

"Okay."

"So, back then, a building this large served more than one purpose. The upstairs floors were still courtrooms, and the basement served as holding cells," he said.

"You mean the jail?" I felt relieved.

"Okay, so yeah," Remy said and ran his hand through his hair. "That, but there's a reason I called it holding cells instead of the jail. They didn't just use them for criminals. Back then there was nowhere to put the severely mentally ill." He waited for my reaction.

"Tell her the rest," Toto said softly as the doors opened.

"Yeah, tell me the rest," I said as we stepped off the elevator.

"So that's what one-half of the basement was used for. The other half was a morgue."

"A morgue? In the courthouse?" For a moment, I thought he was messing with me, but the look on his face was completely serious.

"Yeah, so this wasn't just a courthouse and a jail. Back then, there wasn't a hospital anywhere around here. If they had a disease outbreak or something where there were a lot of hurt or sick people, they also used this building for that. Even when they weren't using any of the courthouse as a hospital, they still needed a cold, dark place to store people who died. That was the basement."

"And that doesn't bother you?" I asked. "You work down here all alone."

"Old buildings have their quirks," he said with a shrug.

"Where does Chris want to start?" I asked.

"Once we get the film of him getting off the elevator, he wants to start in the old morgue section. If that's okay with you?" Link asked Remy.

"Sure, the room is in the back. It's not very big. Nothing like you'd find in a modern hospital or anything like that," he said. "It was full of boxes when I took over the archives, but I moved them all out. It seemed disrespectful."

I wasn't sure what to expect, but despite an unsettled feeling in the air, the morgue wasn't as bad as I'd thought. There were two large metal tables, and I couldn't be sure if they were used for bodies at some point or if they were just old metal tables. The whole room was dingy white tile.

The only thing that was slightly alarming was an old metal cabinet with four huge drawers. It looked like a small version of the drawers you see in the horror movies where there's a morgue.

"You all right?" Remy asked.

"Yeah. I just wasn't expecting that," I said and pointed at it.

"It's empty," he said with a chuckle.

"I figured that," I said and smacked him on the arm playfully. "I just didn't realize this place was used as a morgue recently enough that there would be a... body refrigerator."

"It's pretty old. If that makes you feel any better," he said. "Forty or fifty years maybe."

"Let's get some footage of the room," Chris said. "I know you guys can't leave us, but could you wait in the doorway? Unless you'd like to be on the show? We could still arrange that."

"No, that's okay," I said as Remy and I retreated to the doorway.

We stood and watched as the Ghost Seekers conducted their investigation. First Chris talked about the history of the courthouse and relayed all of the stuff Remy had told me in the elevator to the camera. Except his version included a great deal more detail.

When he was done with his segment, they went to Rachel doing her EVP. She must have had a list of questions she normally asked, and I watched with great attention as Rachel recited them.

Is there anyone here with us?

Does anyone wish to communicate?

Is there anything you want to say?

I shivered after she asked the third question. "Did you turn the air conditioning up in here?" I whispered to Remy.

The Ghost Seekers all swiveled around to look at me. "It's okay, we'll edit it out," Link said. "Not a problem."

"But she's right," Rachel said. "It's really cold in here all of a sudden. Bobby, what are you getting on the EMF?"

"It's elevated a little," he said.

Just then, a breeze blew through the door and then rattled on of the drawers that wasn't closed all the way. "Did you hear that?" Bobby asked.

"Hear it? Did you feel that?" Rachel asked. "Go over by the drawer," she said to Bobby. "Get a reading over there."

"It was probably just a gust of wind from the elevator shaft. Someone probably came through the front doors and wind came down from there."

"Oh, man," Bobby said. "The EMF is going nuts."

"It's probably just something with the electricity," Remy said. "It's older in this part of the building."

"Get in a drawer," Rachel said.

"What?" Chris asked.

"I meant Bobby," she said. "Bobby needs to get in one of the drawers. Maybe one of the spirits will communicate with him. I'll lie on one of the tables."

"You guys, no," I said.

"It's cool. We've done this before. We did it at that old abandoned hospital in Alabama," she said. "The ratings on that episode were through the roof. Get in the drawer, Bobby."

"Chris?" I hoped he'd talk some sense into them.

"It's okay. We have done this before. We won't close the drawer all the way."

The idea seemed completely crazy to me, but if Chris thought it was okay, I decided to just let it go. Even if a spirit attacked, and I doubted one would, Remy and I could protect the crew without being too obvious.

"Does someone else want to get in the drawer this time?" Bobby asked.

It was dark in the room, but I could tell he looked a little pale. He'd been so angry and audacious before that I hadn't expected him to look so frightened.

"I'll do it," Chris said. "Bobby, you keep taking EMF readings. Toto, make sure you get the footage of me going into the drawer and Rachel doing EVP questions while she's on the table. We'll film for fifteen minutes and hopefully get something that's at least a little exciting for when we edit it down."

I watched as Rachel climbed up onto one of the tables and Chris pulled out one of the drawers. He lay down in it and gave a thumbs-up before telling the camera he hoped that one of the spirits inhabiting the courthouse would reach out to him. He said he wanted them to make him understand what it was like for them.

Rachel began asking the same questions she'd asked before. She asked new questions too about whether the spirit was alone, how many there were, and why they were lingering in the old morgue.

I couldn't sense any ghosts, and none were manifesting. I was glad of that. I knew the black-eyed specter I'd seen on the top floor would have been ten times as scary down in that basement, but the fifteen minutes passed without much happening. The EMF reader read a little higher when Chris climbed in the drawer, but that could be explained away.

They did the same thing in the jail cells and then again when we went upstairs to the courtrooms. "Surely someone was sentenced to hang in one of these courtrooms," Rachel said. "That's what they did, right?"

No one answered her, but when the others had wandered off a little way, I tried to slip a question in without seeming too obvious. "Were things all right between you and Kurt?"

"I don't see how that's any of your business," she said.

"I guess it's not, but I was just curious. You two didn't seem very close. I was just wondering if that's because you hadn't been together very long or because you were having problems."

"We'd been together for three years," she said. "That's probably why we didn't seem lovey-dovey enough for you."

"I'm not accusing you of anything," I said. "I'm just worried that something drove Kurt to hurt himself." I didn't believe he'd hurt himself, but I wanted to diffuse the situation.

"Yeah, a ghost drove him to kill himself. One of those witches that was hung at your house. It was revenge for us poking around."

"You have no way of knowing that," I said. "Besides, have you ever heard of a case of a ghost possessing someone and pushing them to suicide?"

"Yes, of course I've heard of it before. In my line of work, it's not even that unusual. We get calls all of the time from people who think a loved one was possessed before they killed themselves."

It was a sad thought, and for a moment it took my breath away. But I didn't believe it was ghosts possessing people. Maybe those people had been afflicted by dark spirits, but I didn't think there was an epidemic of angry ghosts walking around making people off themselves.

"How did they know?" I asked.

Rachel looked at me stunned for a moment. I could tell she wasn't used to anyone questioning her.

"They knew that something wasn't right because of the way the person started to behave. They'd become nervous and jumpy, and then their physical health would start to fail. Most of them said it wasn't anything serious, but a sort of low-level malaise that the person couldn't shake. Some of them complained about hearing or seeing things right before the end, and a few even began experiencing phenomenon like waking up with bites or scratches."

"I'm no expert in the occult or anything, but I've seen plenty of horror movies," I said. "That sounds like demons, not ghosts."

"You're really going to suggest that you know more than me about this stuff because you've seen some horror movies?" she scoffed and then walked away to join Bobby before I could say anything else.

I wanted to tell her that I thought I knew more than her because I was a witch and had control of the forces of nature and magic. But that would have been a bit of a stretch. Oh, and I would have been violating the norms that said I couldn't tell random humans about the Coventry witches.

"You think it was her?" Remy asked when he joined me.

"I don't know. She's pretty dark and also arrogant. But how could she have done it? Rachel's got a big mouth, but she's kind of small. I can't see how she could have gotten him into that tree and killed him without magic, and she's definitely not a witch."

The rest of their investigation was completely uneventful until we went outside. The ghoulish specter that haunted the top floor of the courthouse remained hidden while we were inside, but per her usual routine, she showed up when we were outside in front of the courthouse.

Chris was talking about the locations of the town's whipping post when I saw her. Of course, I wasn't subtle about it. How could you blame me? She startled me even though I knew to expect her. Just before I turned my head to see if anyone else had noticed, what I thought had to be a contemptuous smile, it was hard to tell from that distance for sure, spread across her face.

The Ghost Seekers all looked where I was looking, and Chris let out an audible gasp. "Get that on camera."

She disappeared nearly as soon as Toto swung the camera away from Chris and pointed it at the courthouse. "She's gone," Toto said.

"Did you get her? Did you get anything at all? Even one frame of her would be something. That's all we need," Chris said.

"I don't know. Let me look," Toto said.

I held my breath as everyone gathered around for the playback. He did catch a glimpse of her just before she vanished, but it wasn't anything too convincing. More importantly, it wasn't proof of magic.

"Let's go back up there," Chris said. "Do we have time?"

I looked at my phone. "We have about a half hour before they said we have to be out. You want to drag everything back up there?"

"Of course, I do," Chris said with a laugh. "You saw that too. I know you did."

"All right. Let's go," I said with a sigh.

I was nervous the whole time that the specter was going to appear in plain sight or worse. She did not. There was nothing more than a rattling sound that could have been a secretary opening a stuck file cabinet drawer and some cold spots that could have been the building's air conditioning kicking on.

Still, when we left, the Ghost Seekers seemed happy. "So that hunt was successful?" I asked Chris as we walked out to our parked vehicles.

"Oh, yeah, totally. You might not have thought it was much because you live in a place where that kind of activity is commonplace, but for us, Coventry has been a boon." He suddenly lost his excited edge and grew sullen. "For a second, I forgot he was gone."

"It's okay," I said. "I'm sure that's going to happen a lot."

"He'd be proud of what we did today. Kurt would have been so excited to see this."

"I mean, I'm sure he probably can, right?" I asked.

"You know, I hadn't thought about it that way," Chris said. "I hope he's not hanging around to see the show. I hope he moved on to heaven or whatever. Do you believe in heaven? I guess I never asked what your thoughts are on all this ghost stuff."

For the briefest moment, I wondered if I could get away with holding a séance to communicate with Kurt's spirit. The last one hadn't gone so well, but that didn't mean it wasn't possible. Perhaps if I'd let the Ghost Seekers get a room at Mother Hattie's Inn, Annika, Remy, and I could have done it with Meri's help. As it stood, I'd have to shelve the thought. There was no way I could do it with them around. We'd have to wipe their memories and their equipment.

"I do believe there is something else," I said as noncommittally as I could. "More importantly, I believe you'll see your friend again someday." I just hoped that someday wasn't while they were in Coventry with their cameras rolling.

Chapter Seven

I was about to get into Remy's car to leave when someone shouted, "Hey, you."

Most of the Ghost Seekers weren't in their van yet. Everyone but Toto was standing outside putting equipment in the back. Toto sat in the passenger seat reviewing the footage on his camera again.

We all turned to see who was calling out to us. At first, I just thought it was Annika. It wasn't quite time for Annika to close up yet, but perhaps she'd decided to lock up the shop and head over to my house early.

But it wasn't Annika. It was a woman I'd seen around town, but I hadn't met. She had a furious look on her face as she crossed the square in our direction.

"Can I help you?" Remy called out and took a step in front of me.

I didn't know if he picked up on danger from her or if he was just being protective. Either way, it was an interesting gesture.

"I want to talk to her," she said and pointed a thin finger at me.

"What?"

"Everyone knows about what happened at that house this morning. You shouldn't be allowed to live there. No one should have access to that place. The town should have torn it down when your crazy aunt was hauled off to the asylum. Or we should have burned it down," she spat.

"Helen, stop it," Remy said. "You need to go, or I'm going to call the sheriff. You are skirting the line of threatening my friend, and I won't allow it."

Helen, her name according to Remy, recoiled for a second, but then she narrowed her eyes at him. "You," she said and pointed at Remy. "I know what you are. I know what all of you are. You don't scare me!"

"Helen," a voice rang out from the other side of the square.

It was Amelda. She'd come out of the library and was quickly making her way down the stone steps. If Helen recoiled when Remy rebuked her, she looked absolutely stricken at the sight of Amelda heading her way.

"Helen," Amelda said as she approached. "If you have a problem with my family, you need to take it up with me."

"Amelda, I don't have a problem with anyone in your family. I'm addressing her," she said and pointed at me.

"Really, because I see a member of my family standing there," Amelda said.

"I'm not talking to Remy," Helen said softly.

"Are you arguing with me?" Amelda asked calmly.

"No. I mean. No, Amelda. I'm sorry," Helen said and turned to walk away.

As soon as Helen was leaving, Amelda turned and retreated to the library without another word. Remy offered a shrug, and I shrugged back.

"Looks like someone else buys into your story," Bobby said to Rachel.

I turned around and caught her glaring at him. "It's not a story, stupid. There's something about this *place*."

"We're going to head over to that pizza place and grab some dinner. You're invited," Chris said, "But I also wanted to give you some breathing room before the investigation begins if you want. We're not going to do any ghost hunting, so I think we can manage without you for a while."

"Thanks for the invite," I said. "I think I will just go home for a bit. Thorn is supposed to be coming over for a while after work."

"Cool, see you in a couple of hours then."

When Remy was halfway back to my house, he said, "I can just drop you off."

"No," I said. "Thorn's supposed to be coming over, but you don't have to leave. Just eat with us. I need you there tonight for their investigation."

"Really, Brighton. I can make myself scarce for a couple of hours if you want alone time with him."

"Do you want to leave? Is that why you're pushing, because if you've got somewhere else you'd rather be, just say it."

"No, that's not it," he said, and I saw the slightest hint of blush color his cheeks.

It took me back to when we met.

"Good, then you're coming in and we're all having dinner together. I'm sure Annika will show up anyway, and Brody is there unless he wandered off somewhere."

As soon as we walked through the front door, Meri appeared. "Really? You turned them into goats without me?"

"No. They're at the pizza place getting dinner. They'll be here to do their investigation when they're done."

"And they didn't invite you? That's rude. We should turn them into something worse than goats... Spam maybe."

"They did invite me, but I wanted to come home and be with you," I said in sing-song voice.

"Oh, shut up," Meri said as he turned to sashay out of the room.

"Wait, don't go. I want to give you all the hugsy wugsies," I said and chased after him.

Meri hissed and darted off to find one of his wall holes. I laughed and went to the kitchen to get a Diet Coke.

"That wasn't very nice," Remy teased.

"Oh, he's fine," I said.

"But he hissed at you. I've never seen him do that before."

"Me neither, but he didn't try to turn me into an animal or a canned lunch meat product. I assume we'll have made up by dinner."

"You turned them into goats without me?" Meri walked through the kitchen doorway.

Remy and I looked at each other. "Meri? Are you okay?"

"I mean, I'm a little miffed that you turned the Ghost Squeakers into goats without me, but other than that, I'm right as rain."

"Um, we just had this conversation ten seconds ago," I said.

"Well, now, that's impossible because I was upstairs in the library with your brother," he said. "So what's for dinner?"

"Meri, we just had a conversation with a cat that looked just like you," I said and waited for it to sink in.

"Crap," he said. "Where did it go?"

"Into one of your wall holes," I said. "I think that one."

"You guys hang out. I've got this," Meri said. "You might want to go outside."

"Okay, but what about Brody?"

"He's in the attic. I'm sure it's fine."

While we were outside, I found myself wandering over to the tree. I looked up into its branches as I looked for... Actually, I wasn't sure what I was looking for.

"Hold still," Remy said. "Don't move."

"What's wrong?" I said, but I froze.

"Look down at the ground," he said.

I looked down, and I wasn't sure what I was seeing at first. "Oh, there are so many footprints," I said. "But they could have just been from Thorn and the coroner."

"That could be, but look," Remy said. "They go all the way around the tree."

"That is odd. It could have been Thorn or the coroner, but I don't know why they would have walked all the way around the tree."

"It's not proof, but it is evidence that someone might have... assisted him in getting up in that tree."

"Well, if the coroner believes he hanged himself, then what? Someone either strangled him or broke his neck. I need to find out which," I said.

"Why?"

"Because we need to know if he was strangled with the rope or if we have to be on the lookout for someone strong enough to break his neck."

"You could try asking Thorn if he could find out from the coroner," Remy said.

"He's supposed to come for dinner. I can ask him then."

"What are we going to do about the Ghost Seekers and their investigation of Hangman's House if Thorn is here?" Remy asked. "You think he'll be okay hanging out and watching them work?"

"I don't think he'll stay after dinner," I said. "He'll probably have to get back to his daughter. Perhaps if he doesn't, I'll gently make that suggestion."

"You're going to tell him to leave?" Remy seemed surprised.

"In another couple of days, this will all be over. I'm sure things will get straightened out then. For now, I'm just going to keep my head up and manage everything as best I can."

It turned out that I wouldn't have to worry about it after all. We saw Meri in the widow and assumed we could go back in.

"How do we know it's him?" Remy asked as he closed the front door behind us.

"Isn't there some sort of witchy test we can do? Like, we can just use magic, right?"

"I'm right here," Meri said.

"Sorry, we just want to make sure it's you. That thing mimicking you was pretty convincing."

"Whatever," Meri said and jumped up on the sofa.

"Yeah, I think that's him," I said.

"Just one second," Remy said.

Remy waved his hands in front of him, muttered some incantation that I couldn't really understand, and Meri began to glow blue. My familiar flicked his tail a few times in annoyance.

"Hey, can you turn this off? I'm trying to get a nap in before the Ghost Squeakers come back."

"It's him," Remy said. "One hundred percent."

Just then, Thorn called. Something had come up with Dani, and he wasn't going to be able to make it to dinner.

"That's okay," I said. "Hey, before you go. You can answer one question for me. Um... Do you know, or can you find out, if Kurt died because of strangulation or a broken neck?"

"Why do you need to know that?" he asked, and I could almost hear his eyebrow shoot up.

"I just do. I think there are more footprints outside around the tree than can be explained," I said.

"I don't know that, Brighton, because the coroner ruled it a suicide. I didn't get any further information."

"Can you ask her? Could you maybe call her and just ask?"

"I'm not going to do that, Brighton. She ruled it a suicide. I know it's probably traumatic because it happened at your house, but you've got to drop this."

"I just...."

"Look, Dani needs me right now. I've got to go. I love you, and I'll call you as soon as I can."

Thorn hung up before I could get another word in. He didn't even wait for me to say *I love you too*. Maybe it was because he knew, or maybe it was because it didn't matter.

"You all right?" Remy asked.

"I'm fine."

"Whoa," he said.

"Hey, we've probably got an hour or so before the Ghost Seekers get here to do the investigation. You want to get into some trouble with me?"

"Yeah, of course," Remy said with a smile.

"You don't even know what it is."

"Doesn't matter. Whatever it is, I'm here for it," he said.

Chapter Eight

It took us about fifteen minutes to drive to the coroner's office. That gave us a half hour inside and then fifteen minutes to get back to Hangman's House if I wanted to stay on the hour timeline.

"You sure you want to don this?" Remy asked as I pulled my car into the parking spot furthest from the back of the building.

"Are you chickening out now?" I teased.

"Not at all," he said. "But you should have let me drive."

"We're not going to get caught," I said. "But if we did, I don't want you taking the fall for this. It was my idea."

"Okay," he said. "When we get out, I'll put a cloaking spell over the car. We go in, we find the information we need, and then we come back out. The farther away I get from your car and the longer I have to hold the spell, the harder it will be."

There were no other cars in the coroner's office parking lot. As I'd suspected, everyone else had gone home for the day. There were no security cameras on the outside of the building, and I suspected there wouldn't be any inside either.

Maybe in the big city they had all kinds of technology, but we were in a fairly rural area. The coroner's office was one town over from Coventry, but Langdon was an even smaller town that Coventry. It had been the county seat at one time, hence why the office was located there.

Remy easily popped the lock on the back door with a touch of magic. We went inside and looked around for security cameras, but as I'd suspected, there were none. Their philosophy on security was probably something like *who would break into a morgue that's practically in the middle of nowhere?*

There were always those people who had... romantic feelings toward the dead, but I doubted that was much of a problem in our little county. And if it was, I chose not to think too deeply about it.

"Any idea where the bodies might be?" I asked.

"How about we look for files." Remy narrowed his eyes.

Great – I thought. I was the weirdo.

"I just thought maybe the file was near the body," I said defensively.

"You're right," he said with a chuckle. "The file might be there with the body."

"So do you think it's in the basement? Does this place have a basement?"

"Only one way to find out."

The building did have a basement, and not surprisingly, it was where the body was kept. There was an office on one side and cold storage on the other.

There were no files anywhere, but there was a computer. Lockers lined one wall of the office, and when I looked inside, I found boxes containing the deceased's belongings.

"I'm going to try and find his stuff," I said.

"I'll look for files on the computer," Remy said.

"Hey, that's a good plan. I bet even in a small place like this, most of the records are electronic now."

A few minutes later, I found the locker with Kurt's things. I took the box out and went through it as gingerly as possible. It felt invasive to be going through his things, and I wanted to be as respectful as possible.

"So you want to know?" Remy asked.

"Yeah, what is it?"

"He died from strangulation. His neck wasn't broken."

"Oof."

"The coroner's notes say it looked like he struggled against the rope as there were marks up and down his neck. Possibly because he changed his mind."

"He wasn't struggling against the rope because he changed his mind," I said as I moved Kurt's pants to one side of the box. "He was struggling against the person trying to kill him."

Underneath everything was a plastic baggie with Kurt's phone in it. I took it out of the box and then out of the bag. It had a fingerprint reader on the back, but a little magic was all it took to open the phone. It still had a charge.

If going through his clothes felt like an intrusion, going through his phone was ten times worse. Still, I reasoned that I was trying to help him. If Remy and I didn't figure it out, his killer would never meet justice.

I went right for his text messages, and what I found wasn't shocking. He and Rachel had been having problems. In fact, they'd nearly broken up right before showing up in Coventry. Kurt was especially upset the night before he died when Rachel took off after Bobby.

"What is it?" Remy startled me.

"It seems as though he and Rachel were having problems."

"She's so tiny, though. There's no way she dragged him up into that tree," Remy said. "Maybe if she was a witch, but she's not."

Before I could respond, we heard a door slam shut somewhere in the building. I quickly began putting Kurt's things back into the box while Remy shut the computer down.

"Do you think we can get out without being seen?" I whispered.

"I don't know who would be here," Remy said.

"Maybe someone forgot their wallet or something," I said. "I hope no one called the cops."

"I don't think anyone called the cops," he said. "They would have had to follow us in here to know we're here."

"Unless someone who works here is a witch, and they came back because they forgot their wallet," I said.

"Let's just get out of here."

We snuck up the stairs, and Remy poked his head out of the stairwell to see if anyone was around. Nobody was in the tiny lobby area, but we could hear someone down the hall moving around.

"Maybe we should just wait until they go?" I whispered.

"What if they go downstairs for some reason?" he whispered back.

"Hello?" the person down the hall called.

"Crap, go," I said, and we made a break for it.

I heard the person call out "hello" again as I softly closed the back door behind us. We sprinted for my car and dove in like the mob was after us.

Remy barely had his seatbelt buckled, and I was whipping the car out of the parking space and peeling out of the lot.

"That was close," he said once we were on the road.

"Do you think they saw us?" I asked.

"The car was still invisible until we got out of the lot," he said, "but I'm going to need a cheeseburger or something. That took a lot out of me."

"We'll get some on the way back. Why don't you call in a to-go order to the diner?" I said.

Remy got two cheeseburgers, and he ate one of them in the car on the way back. I wasn't sure I'd be able to eat mine when we got back to my house. Something I'd seen at the diner had shaken me to my core. As soon as we pulled up out front, Remy volunteered to go in.

"No, it's okay. I can do it," I said.

"No, really. I'll go," Remy insisted.

That was when I looked up and saw why he wanted to go in. Thorn had said he could come over because something had come up with Dani. I discovered what that was. He was inside the diner with his daughter, and a woman I could only assume was his ex-wife. I immediately scooted down the seat and hid so Thorn wouldn't be able to see me if he looked out the window.

"What are you doing?" Remy asked. "Why are you hiding? You have no reason to hide."

"Please go get the food. Please hurry," I said.

I had no idea why, but the notion of seeing Thorn while he was with his ex-wife and daughter turned my stomach a little. It was probably anxiety and a little anger too.

He wasn't exactly straightforward with me about what he was doing. If he had been, I would have understood. The fact that he hid it caused me concern, but I didn't want to deal with it right then.

So Remy hurried in, picked up the food, and we were off. When we got home, Brody's car was in a different spot. He'd gone to pick up Annika from work, and fortunately, they'd gotten their own dinner because Remy and I hadn't grabbed anything for them.

"Any word on the Ghost Seekers?" Annika asked.

"They were going out for pizza and should be back any time," I said.

"Where were you guys?" she tried to ask casually.

I looked over at Remy and he shrugged. "We were at the coroner's Office. We broke in to find out exactly how Kurt died."

"Oh," Annika said. "Did you find out?"

"We did. It was strangulation."

"Ooohhh. So he really could have been murdered."

"Yeah," I said.

"Good job. I've taught you well," she said with a chuckle.

"Wait, you got her into doing this?" Brody asked.

"I'm a bad influence. What can I say?" Annika countered.

Chapter Nine

The Ghost Seekers arrived a little while later. Bobby smelled like beer and was being sullen and withdrawn. Rachel was keeping her distance from him too, and that was unusual. I wondered if he was taking Kurt's death hard because the two of them hadn't been able to reconcile.

I was in the living room when Chris, Link, and Toto went upstairs to begin filming. Bobby trailed behind them and made a snarky comment about getting some camera time.

Rachel went the other way into the kitchen. I didn't want to follow right behind her because it would have seemed creepy, but I also didn't want her poking around the house alone. Thankfully, Meri went after her.

"I'm going to go upstairs," Annika said.

"I'll come with you. I need to make sure my room is spotless in case they wander in there," Brody added.

"Thank you for this," I said to my brother. "Thank you for not getting upset about them doing this investigation."

"It's your house," he said. "She left it to you. I'm just a guest."

With that, Annika and Brody went upstairs to keep an eye on the crew. That left Remy and I in the living room.

I waited a few minutes and then went into the kitchen to see what Rachel was doing. She had her recorder out and was whispering questions.

When I went into the kitchen, she turned to look at me but did not stop what she was doing. She'd ask a question then stop, rewind the recording, and listen. So far, Rachel hadn't picked up anything.

"Don't you have to speed up or slow down the recordings sometimes?" I asked.

That was one thing I remembered from an article I'd read at some point about ghost hunting. People would hear EVP when they slowed the recording down.

"I think what those people are hearing is just their mind picking up on something that's not there," she said.

"But you get recordings that you can just play back?"

"You hear things sometimes. Whether it's really the voice of a ghost or the power of suggestion, I don't know."

"So you don't really believe that a ghost possessed Kurt."

"I didn't say that. All I said was that I don't know if this EVP stuff is real, but it plays well for the cameras. The viewers at home want to believe, so it's easy to get them to hear things."

"You know he didn't break his neck when he died."

"What?"

"I said I wonder if he broke his neck when he died?" I said. "I wonder if it was instant or if he suffered."

"That's not what you said."

"It is." I kept my face as calm as possible.

"Why are you goading me about him? What are you trying to do?" Rachel put the recorder in her pocket and took a step toward me.

"I'm not trying to goad you." I was. "I'm just wondering if his spirit is still around. The more violent the death, the more likely there will be a haunting, right?"

"I'm going to go join the guys and see if I can get some more camera time for this episode," she said and brushed past me.

Chapter Ten

Later in the evening, the crew took a break to get a drink and rest. Nothing had really happened, but I'd mostly expected that. The house seemed like it would protect me aside from the demons in the basement.

"I think we're going to go down into the basement next," Chris said right on cue.

"What?" I should have seen it coming.

"I promise that Bobby isn't going to draw any pentagrams on the floor, but we have to get some footage in your basement. Please, Brighton." Chris steepled his hands together like he was begging.

"All right," I said. "And then you guys are done, right?"

"We're done here," Chris said, "but we're going to the cemetery across the road after this. We want to make sure we're there for the witching hour."

"Awesome," I said and offered him a huge cheesy smile.

Everyone else got up and started to go down to the basement. The Ghost Seekers anyway. Annika and Brody were hanging out in the living room in front of the fire. Remy and I were still at the kitchen table when Chris turned around and sat back down with us.

"We'll be leaving soon," Chris said. "I just wanted to make sure that I thanked you."

"You're welcome," I said. "I'm sorry that we met the way we did, though. I'm sorry that Coventry wasn't a happy stop for you guys."

"Well, if nothing else," Chris began, "I wouldn't have even had my own show if we hadn't come here. I would have always been in the background."

"Oh," I said because I wasn't sure what else to say.

"I'm sorry. That must have sounded awful. It's one of those things that just slips out before you have a chance to really think about what it means," he said and stood up. "I'm going to go downstairs with the crew. Will you two be joining us?"

"Yes," I said. "We will. Remy?"

I hadn't spent much time in the basement. Mostly just going down there to use the washer or dryer and then running back up to the kitchen as quickly as possible.

For some reason, demons liked to manifest down there, but I had no idea where they came from. Since they didn't appear anywhere else in the house, I'd tried to ignore it as much as possible.

The remaining crew of the Ghost Seekers, along with Meri, were down in the basement. My familiar sat on top of the washing machine observing the group he called the Ghost Squeakers, but none of them paid him any mind. Little did they know; he was the one creature who could save their lives and probably their immortal souls too. I wasn't quite clear on that one, but they were demons.

Remy, Annika and I stood back and watched as the Ghost Seekers made their way through the darkish, but ambiently lit with stage lighting, basement. Chris talked some more about the history of the house and what could have been lurking there.

Toto occasionally filmed Rachel doing EVP while Link's camera flashed at an attempt to catch spirit photography. Bobby appeared to just be looking around.

In fact, at one point, he wandered off into a side room that I didn't even know was there. I hadn't gone that far into the basement, but he found what Chris assumed, for the camera, was an old fruit cellar.

Along the back wall was a boarded-up section. "Cut the camera," Chris said when he spotted it. "What is that?"

He turned to look at me, but all I could offer was a shrug. For whatever reason, I hadn't been that far in the basement. There could have been millions of dollars in pirate treasure down there and I would have never known.

"There's a breeze coming from behind it," Rachel said. "It's a doorway to somewhere."

"We have to open it up," Chris said. "You seriously didn't know this was here?"

"I don't come down here much, and I don't go past the washer and dryer," I said.

"You're going to let us open this up, right?" Chris asked. "You have to. This is huge. Don't you want to know what's in there?"

I didn't want to know, but I supposed I should. Remy was shooting me a warning look, but honestly, if it was going to be opened, I'd rather when there were tons of people around. I temporarily forgot that if there was something hideous in there, we'd have to use our powers in front of humans. I embraced the comfort of having so many people around without thinking.

"Okay," I said.

"Do you have a hammer somewhere?" Link asked. "Or perhaps a crowbar?"

"I need to see if I have a toolbox," I said. "Perhaps out in the shed. Give me a minute."

I went outside to check the shed while everyone else in the basement waited. Sure enough, there was a toolbox out there with a hammer. I took it back into the house.

"Let me do it," Link said, and I handed him the hammer. "I was a carpenter before I joined the show."

For a moment the breath caught in my throat, but then I remembered that Meri's spell would have told me if Link was actually Grey. Besides, Link had been with the Ghost Seekers, there was no way he could be Grey.

Unless Grey killed Link and is masquerading.

I pushed the thought aside and had faith that Meri's spell would protect us.

My thoughts were interrupted as the sound of Link tearing away the first board hit my ears. We all stood around and watched for a few minutes as Link tore the rest of the wood down.

Behind it was an opening in the wall, a dark chasm that seemed to go on much farther than an auxiliary fruit cellar.

"Is that a tunnel?" Toto was the first to ask.

"It can't be," I said. "That's crazy. It's got to just be a root or fruit cellar."

Chris shined a flashlight into it. "I can't see the back of it." He swept the light from side to side. "But you can see the walls. Looks like a tunnel to me."

"I can't believe it," Remy said. "I had no idea they went to any of the houses."

"You knew about this?" I asked him.

"I didn't know about this particular tunnel, but I knew they were under the town," he said. "But most of them are condemned. No one goes in them anymore."

I knew he meant there were tunnels under the courthouse, and that's why he'd said it. He was letting me know why he hadn't told us, and Remy was explaining to the Ghost Seekers why they couldn't go in the ones under the places they were visiting.

"Let's see what's in there," Bobby said and started down the dark corridor.

"Bobby, wait," Chris said, but he followed him.

Toto went too with the camera raised. "I'm going to get it all."

"Guys, wait," I said, but they were completely enrapt by the tunnel.

I was curious too, so I followed along. Remy was behind me. When I looked back, Meri sat at the opening watching us. I wasn't sure how far he would follow, but I knew he intended to protect us.

The tunnel went on far beyond the edges of my house and my property. It branched off in several places too, but every time we came to a spot that might have connected to tunnels under other buildings, it was sealed off. Not with wooden boards either. Someone had taken the time and effort to cut the Hangman's House tunnels off from the rest with concrete walls.

There also seemed to be no paranormal activity in the tunnels. A strange breeze coming from somewhere was the closet thing. I'd hoped that we'd find the source of the demons in there so that I'd at least know where they were coming from, but we didn't find that. That was probably a good thing considering the Ghost Seekers were with us.

Eventually, the crew decided that they had enough footage to cobble together a show. None of them wanted to spend any more time in the tunnels, and they didn't want to spend another night in the house either.

Their hope was that if they spent the night at Mother Hattie's Inn, they might accidently catch something. Since they weren't going to do any active ghost hunting, I didn't think I needed to babysit them overnight. I also understood why they didn't want to be in the house. It seemed like Kurt's death was finally beginning to sink in for many of them.

It was an uneventful night for me too. I sat by the fire reading while Meri curled up next to me. Remy stayed the night too. While I sat reading, he did the same on the other end of the sofa. It was a quiet night of comfortable companionship.

Brody took Annika out to see a movie. They both insisted it wasn't a date, but who was I to judge? My own love life was a mess. If they could be happy, then who was I to stand in the way? I thought it was too soon after Brody's loss, but maybe he and Annika could have something real. I knew that sometimes, that's the only thing that can soothe the pain.

I woke up the next morning and there was a heaviness in my chest that I hadn't expected. Before I could even pick my head up off the pillow, I was in tears. The weight of everything that was happening with Thorn hit me hard. Kurt's death had kept me from thinking about it too much, but when I was alone in the early hours of the morning, I couldn't hide from it anymore.

Something was broken, and I knew it couldn't be fixed. I wanted to rip the Band-Aid off as fast as possible, so I decided that while everyone was sleeping, I'd do a reverse love spell on myself. It felt like the only way to heal.

There was a note in the kitchen from Remy that he'd left early to get ready for work. It was nice of him to be so considerate. He didn't have to leave me notes telling me where he was and telling me he hoped I was able to have a wonderful day. I checked my phone, and sure enough, there were no messages from Thorn.

How had I been so stupid?

Tears ran down my cheeks as I thought about how I should have known better. He pulled away whenever there was the slightest bump in the road, but I'd believed his sweet promises. I'd cared more about the chemistry between us than the reality in front of me.

I gathered the candles, salt, herbs, and oils I'd need to do the spell. When I had it all, I grabbed a chunk of rose quartz and another of black tourmaline.

All I had to do was decide where to do my ritual. I wanted to be outside in nature even if that meant it would be harder for me to cast a salt circle. I couldn't get the images of Kurt in the front yard out of my mind, so I went to the back instead.

It occurred to me that I could probably make a circle with fallen tree branches, so I picked up some of those and made myself a small magic ring. Once they were in place, I sprinkled a little bit of salt around the edges. I didn't want to kill the grass, so I didn't use much.

I figured it would be okay since I wasn't summoning anything. After I stuck the long candles into the dirt, I lit them and anointed my forehead with gardenia oil and my wrists with dragon's blood oil. I began the chant I'd made up to reverse my love for Thorn.

Set me free

Was the last thing I remembered...

Next thing I knew, Remy was standing in front of me shaking me. Meri rubbed up against my back and then both of my knees. Remy's face was a mask of fear and anxiety. Meri began to wail a mournful sound.

I could see them and hear them, but it was as if I were looking out at them through glass windows instead of my eyes. I was there but not there.

"Come on, Brighton. Come on, baby," Remy said and shook me again. "You can't do this to me. I need you. I know I said I'd stay back and let you figure things out for yourself, but I shouldn't have done that. I shouldn't have left you adrift. Please. Please wake up." He turned to look at Meri. "How do we get her back? Help me." Remy sounded so desperate, it made my heart hurt even more.

So I tried to get back to myself.

"Wait, she moved," Meri said. "Look."

Just then, I was able to slide back into myself just enough to take Remy's hand.

My other hand slid over Meri's soft head and scratched behind his ear. He instinctively began to purr.

"Yes, baby, yes!" Remy exclaimed, and then his lips made contact with my forehead.

The sensation was like a bomb going off inside of me, and when the dust settled, I was back.

"What happened?"

Instead of answering, Remy scooped me up into his arms and began to carry me toward the house. I felt completely rung out as if I'd just run a marathon, and I let my head loll onto his shoulder.

"I'll put the candles out," Meri said. "I'll be right in."

The next thing I remember was waking up on the sofa with Meri staring at me. "That was dumb," he said.

"Where's Remy?"

"He was in the middle of doing a favor for the mayor when I had to go get him to save your butt. He ran back to the courthouse to deliver the files he'd promised. He'll be right back. I'm here to keep an eye on you."

"A judgmental eye," I said and sat up.

"Well, I mean..."

"I know. I just wanted to end it."

"What?" Meri was shocked.

"Not like that. I meant end my feelings for Thorn. I'm so tired of it. I know what's good for me, but it's so hard to do the right thing with stupid feelings in the way," I said.

"So you were trying to do a reverse love spell?" Meri asked. "On yourself?"

"Yeah. I was hoping to leave Remy out of it which is why I was doing it while he was at work. Why didn't you get Annika or Brody?"

"Not that your brother would have been much help, but he sleeps like the dead. Annika is with Amelda, and it was easier to get Remy," Meri said.

"Yeah, I can see that," I said.

"Brighton, are you okay?" Brody said as he came down the stairs.

"Yeah, just a bit of a mishap with a spell. Nothing I can't handle, thanks to Meri," I said.

"Well, I'm going to go out for a jog and then pick up some lunch and take it to Annika," Brody said. "She said she wasn't going to be able to get out for lunch today because of a meeting with her family this morning, so I figured I'd take her something."

"I'll see you later then," I said and offered a wave.

"Probably not until tonight. After lunch with Annika, I've got to go to campus and meet with my advisor."

When he was gone, Meri jumped down and headed for the stairs. "Be right back," he said.

"Wait, I thought you were supposed to watch me," I said.

"Well, if you must know, I need to make a trip to the litterbox," he said. "I'll be right back."

"Oh," I said. "Sorry."

My throat was parched, so I got up and went into the kitchen to get myself a Diet Coke. As I was passing the table, I noticed there was another note on the table on top of Remy's.

Hey, Brighton. Chris here. Sorry I just came into the house, but I knocked and no one answered. I saw you out in the backyard and figured you were busy. I'm downstairs in the tunnels. I found something I think you really need to see. Please come down as soon as you get this.

"Well, that's odd," I said and put the note down.

I didn't really want to go down there by myself, but I was worried about the Ghost Seekers being in the house, and in the basement, without me.

After I grabbed a flashlight, I headed down but left the door open in hopes Meri would know I was down there.

"Hello," I called into the tunnel.

No one answered, so I went further in. I could hear what sounded like someone moving around much further in, but no one would answer when I'd call out.

When the tunnel came to a fork, I strained my ears to hear which direction they were in. I thought I'd picked up the sound of them moving around in the tunnel fork to the right, so I went that way.

I'd only made it a few feet into the tunnel when I felt a hard thump to the back of my head. As I was reaching my hand up and trying to figure out what had happened, I was hit again.

"Hey," I said, but my vision began to swim.

Then, my eyesight started to go out. It turned black around the edges first, and then it was like the tunnel closed around me. My knees went weak, and I slumped to the tunnel floor.

"Really, Brighton," I heard Meri say. "I had to save you again? It's been like fifteen minutes. I just needed to use the litterbox. Jeez."

I sat up and rubbed the back of my head. It was tender, but there wasn't a knot or anything. I'd expected to find one after being hit so hard, but as I started to feel better and better, I realized that Meri had used a healing spell on me.

"Now that you're awake, can you please call Thorn," Meri said.

"For what?"

But as I asked, I could see Bobby and Rachel tied up in the tunnel a few feet ahead of us.

"What's going on?" I asked. "Where's Chris? Why are Bobby and Rachel tied up?"

"Just think about it for a second," Meri said.

Chapter Eleven

As it turned out, the note from Chris was a fake. Bobby and Rachel had snuck into the house and left it while I was in the backyard being catatonic. Meri and Remy had left the door open when they came running through the house to get to me. Whatever I'd done when I'd failed the reverse love spell had weakened the protection wards on the house too.

When I called Thorn, he took them in. While they hadn't confessed to the murder, it looked awfully suspicious that they'd broken into my house. That coupled with the fact that they'd attacked me was enough to encourage the coroner to take another look at the cause of death.

While that happened, they weren't going to get out on bail since they'd been caught in my house. No one questioned how I'd managed to tie them both up. The only issue was that they might not stand trial.

Since they kept raving about how the cat had tied them up using magic, there was the possibility they'd be found incompetent. Whether they went to jail or ended up in a psychiatric facility didn't matter to me. I just wanted them off the streets. It would have been nice to know there'd be justice for Kurt, but public safety was better than nothing.

Chris, Toto, and Link all came by after the arrest. They couldn't believe what had happened. While it was pretty obvious to them, at least after the fact anyway, that Rachel had been cheating on Kurt with Bobby, no one thought it was possible that they'd kill him.

"So that's what you think happened?" Chris asked me. "You think they strangled him and then hung him in the tree." He shivered after he said the last part.

"It seems that way," I said. "I'd almost be willing to put money on it."

"But why try to kill you?" Link asked.

"Because I was investigating it? I wouldn't let it go. They probably thought the only way to get away with the whole thing was to get rid of me," I said.

The part I didn't say was that they didn't know I was a witch and had a powerful familiar. That part had to stay between me and my Coventry family.

"I think I'm going to stick around in Coventry," Link said.

"You are? Why?" I felt bad because the question sounded like I was being short with him. "Sorry, that came out wrong. I'm just curious."

"I don't know," he began. "It feels like home? I think I can get at least a part-time job slinging hash at that Dumbledore place. And I was also a carpenter before. I'm pretty handy with a lot of things."

"Oh, cool. Coventry could probably use that."

"You seem like you could probably use it to."

At first, I couldn't fathom what he was talking about, and then I remembered the garage Grey had left half finished. He was right. I knew it would be nice to have someone finish building it rather than let the half-completed structure sit there to rot.

"You're absolutely right," I said. "Welcome to Coventry, Link. I'm happy to be your first customer."

I want to see you tonight. – The text from Thorn caught me off guard.

I don't know. I've had a rough couple of days. Maybe we should meet for lunch tomorrow or something. – was my response.

Please, Brighton. I'm so sorry. I want to bring Dani to meet you too. I hate to tell you this over text, but I'm ready to get our lives started.

You'd have thought I'd have been over the moon about that revelation, but there was just something sitting in the pit of my stomach about the whole thing. It made me uneasy, but perhaps that was just nerves. I hadn't had much time to think about becoming a stepmother.

Can you come alone at first? I'd like to talk to you before I meet Dani. I think that's best for everyone.

Yes, of course. I can work that out. See you after work, then?

Sure thing. – I said and put the phone aside.

Either way, I did want to meet Dani. She was Thorn's little girl after all, but we had a big discussion to have before that happened. Expectations needed to be managed.

I was a ball of nerves and spent the rest of the afternoon cleaning the house until it gleamed and baking a dozen cupcakes. When it was getting close to being time for Thorn to get off his shift, I went to the fridge to see what I had to make dinner.

Before I could open the fridge, my phone dinged again. I had a feeling I needed to check it before I got my hands dirty.

Sorry, something has come up with Dani and her mom. I won't be able to make it for dinner. Call you later.

Of course.

I felt like I'd given him so much leeway. I thought I'd been understanding. Had I not been super understanding and as supportive as possible?

"I'm going over there," I said.

"Why?" Meri startled me.

"Because this is how I rip the Band-Aid off. Not by casting spells on myself or waiting around for a man to bless me with his appearance to eat the dinner I would have cooked for him."

"I don't know if that's a good idea, but you go get'em, girl," Meri said.

"Whatever."

"Whatever," Meri retorted. "Hey, could you feed me first, maybe?"

I did. I fed Meri, and then I jumped in my car, that started, and drove over to Thorn's house. I pulled into his driveway behind his cruiser and called him because I was too afraid to ring the doorbell.

"What is it, Brighton? I said I'd call you later."

"I'm in your driveway."

"You're what?"

"I'm in your driveway. You need to come talk to me."

"Brighton, this is crazy. I'll call you later."

"I'm in your driveway. I'll be here until you come talk to me," I said and hung up the phone,

Two minutes later, Thorn came out the front door. He was dressed in one of his black t-shirts and a pair of jeans that hung perfectly from his hips yet strained against the bulge of his strong thighs. I said a prayer to the goddess for strength. He was a good-looking man, and it made me a little weak. But I was on a mission.

I got out of the car as he made his way down the driveway. My butt leaned against the driver's door after I closed it, and I pushed back a bad memory about one of the times I'd found the strength to stand up to Donnie.

"What is this about?" he asked, but he looked back over his shoulder.

I followed his line of sight and saw a woman close his front curtain quickly. "You're not alone with Dani," I said.

"I'm not. Her mother is here."

"Then why couldn't you meet me for dinner? Is Dani sick or something?"

"No, she's fine," Thorn said.

He rubbed the back of his neck and refused to make eye contact. I bit my bottom lip to keep from crying, and it worked. I was sad, but not as sad as I'd expected.

"You're getting back together with her, right? That's what this has been about. You trying to decide. You pick me and then you change your mind. So you've been doing it to both of us?"

"Brighton."

"Don't *Brighton* me," I said more forcefully than I expected. "And don't even sweat it, Thorn. I didn't come here to beg you to pick me or anything like that. I didn't invite you over for dinner to work things out in our relationship either. That ship sailed. I wanted to meet your daughter, but I wanted to do it as your friend." It felt good to say it. "Because that's all we'll ever be."

"I don't even think we'll be that," he practically whispered. "We're leaving town."

"What?"

"Sadie, Dani, and I are moving back to the city. Sadie still has her place there, and I called my old boss. I've got a job waiting for me."

"You were just going to leave?"

"I would have come talk to you first. The move is just happening soon, and we had things we needed to work out."

"She's making you leave town fast, so you don't change your mind. Whatever, Thorn. Not my circus."

"Brighton, wait," he said, but his voice held no urgency.

"Wait for what? I'm done waiting."

I got in my car and pulled out of the driveway. He was already back in the house when I hit the gas to drive away. As soon as I was out of sight, the tears came. I cried so hard that I had to pull the car over once, but then something miraculous happened. By the time I got back to my house, the pain had begun to subside. One good cry, and I felt cleansed.

And then I saw it.

Saw him, rather. As I pulled into my driveway, I saw Remy sitting on my front porch waiting for me. It was just like he said, and I felt my breath catch in my throat.

The tears started again as I got out of car, but they were tears of happiness and relief. "Oh, baby, are you okay?" Remy asked. He stood up and rushed to me before pulling me into his arms. "I'm so sorry," he said as he kissed the top of my head. "I should have done more to protect you. I'll never let you down again."

"It's okay," I said. "I'm okay."

"You're okay?" He leaned back and looked at my face. "But you're crying."

"It's good crying," I said. "It really is."

"Good crying?" He let out a chuckle and kissed the top of my head again. "Yay for good crying, I guess."

"You're such a dork," I laughed.

"Hey," he said and tightened the arm around my waist so that I was pulled much closer to him. "I can be alpha if you need it. I can be anything you need." Remy's voice was almost a growl, but he broke into a smile a second later.

"I don't need you to be anything but you," I said and pushed a lock of his hair away from his forehead.

"What you need is to be good and properly kissed by a man who loves you more than anything in this world," he said.

And before I could say another word, he kissed me.

***